IRA FOXGLOVE

Also by Thomas McMahon

Principles of American Nuclear Chemistry: A Novel

McKay's Bees

Loving Little Egypt

IRA FOXGLOVE
a novel

THOMAS McMAHON

brook street press
SAINT SIMONS ISLAND

Brook Street Press
www.brookstreetpress.com

Brook Street Press is a trademark of Brook Street Press LLC

First Edition

Library of Congress Cataloging-in-Publication Data

McMahon, Thomas A., 1943–1999.
    Ira Foxglove / Thomas McMahon.—1st ed.
        p. cm.
    ISBN 0-9724295-3-0
    1.   Scientists—Fiction. 2.   Quests (Expeditions)—Fiction. 3.
Airships—Fiction.   I. Title.

    PS3563.C3858I73 2004
    813'.54—dc22

                                                        2003021792

Art and book design by Kerry Dennehy

Printed in the United States of America

10 9 8 7 6 5 4 3 2 1

Publisher's Note

The publication of *Ira Foxglove* came about in a fashion not dissimilar to the stories found in Thomas McMahon's novels. Start with a little serendipity, add a few interesting coincidences, mix in a loving family, and you have the recipe for how a thirty-year-old unpublished work by an acclaimed writer finds its way to the doorstep of an upstart publishing house.

Like McMahon's previous books, *Ira Foxglove* has an air of gentleness and humor about it. Whimsy is a word that appears over and over in reviews and articles on Thomas McMahon. It's a good word. This accomplished scientist was also a beautiful literary craftsman and it is very unfortunate that this is the last tale we will ever enjoy from a fanciful storyteller and true Renaissance man.

Posthumous publication is not without its challenges. A great deal of dedication has gone into bringing this novel to its intended form by a variety of people, who should be acknowledged: Harriet Wasserman, faithful literary agent; Corlies Smith, master editor; Debra Hudak, project manager; and especially Tom's wife. Each provided invaluable assistance to make the book sing to its fullest.

Brook Street Press is very proud indeed to publish *Ira Foxglove*.

One

Portia left me on a late summer evening. She put all her clothes in two suitcases, carelessly wadding them in. Her tank suit went on top in the small suitcase.

"It's this or go nuts, Ira," she said as she walked out the door.

She had called herself a cab, but it was late coming. I followed her outdoors and sat on the front steps with her until the cab showed up.

"How about this," I suggested. "We'll get floor lamps for every room. Then the place wouldn't be so dark. Then you could stay."

"I don't want to stay."

"I wish you would."

"No," she said.

The cab arrived. It had a black roof and orange fenders. On the side, in black letters, it said DADDY'S CAB.

"You're not going to abandon me in Daddy's Cab, are you?" I asked her.

"I certainly am."

That was her last word. Daddy jumped out, zip, zip, the bags were in, and off they went down Pearl Street. I watched them drive all the way down to the end, then left and out of sight. Aha. The old left turn. This would take them out to Memorial Drive. Another left turn at the traffic circle under the B.U. Bridge, then off to the airport. Portia hadn't told me where she was going, but I imagined I knew. She was going to her sister in New York.

Later, I knew I had played it wrong. I should have been more kind. I should have given her more money. I kept forty dollars in traveler's checks in my chest of drawers. I should have given her that.

This was on Monday. On Wednesday evening, it seemed a reasonable idea to check in with her sister. Portia wasn't there, although she had been. Her sister's husband had loaned her the airfare to England, and she had left earlier that afternoon. I was stupefied.

A week passed without any word. I called Portia's sister again and talked with her for an hour. I've always liked Portia's sister. She's married to a restaurateur who can afford luxuries for her and their children, but she's easy to please and doesn't cost him much. They have a large apartment, and they're generous about sharing it with you when you come to town. They're also generous with food.

Portia's sister hadn't heard anything either, but she didn't mind talking about some of the things Portia had said and done in the brief time she was with them. She had spent nearly all her time in their swimming pool, which was on the roof deck of the building. As this was September and the children of the building were in school, Portia had the pool to herself. Her sister had served Portia all her meals beside the pool, except for dinner, which she had with the family in their eat-in kitchen. After dinner, she was back up in the pool again, under the stars. I've been in this pool after dark, and I know how attractive it can be with the lights of New York reflecting from its moving surface. The Spry sign, for example, comes back inverted and in pieces which break apart and fit together every time a wave passes.

"All that despondent swimming," her sister said. "I was worried about her. I called her on the telephone out on the deck once in a while to see how she was coming along. And I spent a lot of time there with her, too."

"What did she say?"

"She said you were better and didn't need her anymore."

"I am better."

"I'm glad to hear that, Ira," her sister said.

"But that's no reason for her to run away."

"She said the house was too dark. She said you just lie on your back on the couch in the darkness."

"I don't do that all the time. I just do it when my chest is hurting."

"Does it hurt often?"

I thought about this. How much had I been lying around feeling sorry for myself? Enough for Portia and me to fight about it. She wasn't pleased about all that darkness. But I often left the curtains open, so that I could see the street lamp, and a corner of the church against the lighter sky. At twilight in fair weather, this blank brick face of the church would be scarlet, standing on a dark blue sky. On the sidewalk under the street lamp, the adolescents of the neighborhood would fight urgent, sexual, roughhouse games. I could hear them but not see them unless I lifted my head. A girl's scarf would be taken, and the clatter of a running army could be heard moving down the block. When I did lift my head, I would be likely to see a boy pressing a girl against a parked car, keeping her prisoner by his grip on the door handles. But Portia would see only that the parlor was dark and that I was there on the couch, silent.

"It hurts often enough so that I can understand why Portia might be exasperated with me," I said. "I wasn't supposed to have pain this long after my heart attack. I was supposed to be free of pain a month or so after leaving the hospital. Such was not to be."

Portia's sister wanted to stop talking. Her children needed to be put to bed.

"Come on down here and let me take care of you, Ira," she said. "You can float in the pool if the weather stays warm. I know you like that. I'd rather have you here than Portia if you can't be here together. She's too nervous. She swam up and down, up and down, all day long yesterday. Our pool isn't big enough for that. It's more for lying in."

This was a very nice invitation. Portia's sister, like Portia, is a pretty woman. She's two years older than Portia. They're fond of each other.

"I want to come," I told her. "But I want more to be here when Portia writes or comes home. Let's put it off until things are more tranquil."

Months passed. Portia sent me notes on postcards. She treated the abandonment as a joke. On the back of one showing Trafalgar Square she wrote:

It has more cars than this even on
Sunday morning. I can't make up my
mind whether I wish you were here—P

The postcards had no return address, but after the third month I received a letter which led me to understand that she would look for mail at American Express. I wrote to her and sent her all the money in our bank account. In my letter, I asked her what she was doing in London and why she couldn't come home. She answered, on the back of a postcard, that she couldn't explain then but would write me a long letter soon.

Another month passed, and when the letter came, it proved to be very unsatisfactory. It was a vaguely argued manifesto for human wildness. I came close to being referred to in the third person. It was as if Portia was at the end of a long speaking tube, and more interested in letting me know she was there far away, than in saying anything to me I might understand.

More postcards came after that. She described the sights, and once, for a sequence of five cards or so, she pretended to be a rich lady tourist writing to aunts and uncles. She affected an accent and purposely misspelled words. This was also going on as she described visiting Paris, where she spent a few weeks with our eighteen-year-old daughter, Henley, who is enrolled in a school of mime there. Henley wrote me about this visit:

It's great to have Mother here, but she
seems awfully distracted. She wanted me
to join in that game of writing you hick
postcards, but I wouldn't do it.

Meanwhile, my salary as a science teacher at Browning Tech was being strained by the necessity of supporting both Henley and Portia in foreign campaigns. I was forced to borrow even more money than I had when Portia had been home. Although Portia apparently wanted to think about her absence as a practical joke, it had its impractical side.

In late winter, Portia wrote me to say that she was living with a wonderful Indian from Bombay in his flat near King's Cross. Their bed-sitter room had two high windows which looked out on an alley. The skyline was entirely brick chimneys and chimney pots, she said. They had painted each wall of their room a different color. He worked in an administrative job in a government office. Portia was looking for work but meanwhile was putting most of her energy into swimming at the facilities of a nearby school.

She invited me to visit her. She wanted to see me, she said, and her friend had okayed the plan of my living with them for a few days if I would like to come. She suggested that I come during my spring break, a time we had often spent together as a family camping in the White Mountains north of Boston.

I considered Portia's invitation seriously enough to take out a passport and get a smallpox vaccination, but as I thought through my plans, it all began to look too expensive. The most Portia had promised me was a few hours of talk and a chance to meet this guy Dawlish whom she raved about. She had made it clear that I shouldn't expect to bring her back with me. I finally sent her money instead.

I made the decision, as winter was just ending, lying on my bed in the kitchen. The kitchen could be kept warm by using the space heater in the gas stove, thus allowing me to save money by not heating the rest of the apartment. I had tacked Portia's cards and letters on the bulletin board to the right of the stove, just over the foot of my bed. During the winter I had grown into careless habits involving food and had encouraged the cockroaches to exercise their options on future generations years earlier than would have been wise previously. One of my bigger mistakes had been to assume that the spaghetti pot needn't be cleaned between usings. I kept it on the floor under my bed.

A week arrived, during that summer in 1973, of nearly unbearable heat and humidity. The newspapers and broadcast media said that many people in the Northeast thought some kind of end was at hand, since Washington, Philadelphia, and New York were suffocating in a smog blanket each day more and more concentrated in toxins. A quirk of large-scale pressure systems trapped the air over the entire country and held it fixed; there was no wind anywhere for five days. Temperature inversions over the cities sealed them still further. Newspapers published alarms regarding this or that pollution index, including maps with the unhealthy areas of cities indicated in black. Lights flickered and darkened in the late afternoon and evening under the demands of air conditioning. Many people with respiratory diseases were admitted to hospitals.

Boston stewed with the other cities, but faint sea breezes helped it escape serious smog. As in previous summers, I had my usual arrangement with the local school board whereby I was a guard at Browning three nights a week in exchange for the use of a basement laboratory I had assembled there. They also paid me a small salary. Before my heart attack, I would customarily take a daytime job as a consultant at the rubber hose factory on Second Street during the summer months, but not this summer. With only the seven-to-two guard's job to do, I was free to stay in bed during the mornings, but on the week I'm speaking of, it was impossible to lie in bed during the day. On Wednesday of that terrible week, the temperature had already reached ninety-five by ten o'clock, and the humidity was high enough to keep the sun from casting sharp shadows anywhere in the house. I dressed in a cotton shirt and light trousers and stepped out onto the porch, intending to investigate whether the outside could be as bad as the inside.

In my letterbox, there was a fat envelope from Henley. I brought it inside to read it. The letter was long, by her standard. Paris in spring and summer was fantastic, the people at the mime school were beautiful. She was growing as a person. She had just returned from a visit in London with Portia, which Portia had paid for. On returning, she had been given the promise of a job as a cocktail waitress in a bar in the evenings, but until the job started, she was in need of a small loan. Typically, she hadn't stated the amount required, but from the things she needed, including the school's fee, I knew I should send her three hundred dollars. That was three hundred dollars I didn't have. I took off my shoes and socks and lay back on the bed.

Through the windows of the empty bedroom, framed with curtains made (by Portia) of white bed sheets, the scalding glare of the street diffused inside. The bedroom walls, which had been covered with a textured green wallpaper when we moved in, were now painted white, but had become, in Portia's absence, soiled enough to need re-

painting. I looked at my watch. It was just after ten-fifteen.
I picked up the phone and dialed Neptune's number.

"Ira," Neptune said when he answered, "Look, can I
call you back? Where are you?"

"At home."

"O.K. I'll call you in five minutes."

I put a shallow pan of water on to boil. I then went
into the bathroom and used the toilet. (It had a wooden
handle painted violet on the end of the chain.) By the
time I returned to the kitchen, the water was boiling. I
shook in a bit of salt, removed the pan from the flames,
and stirred in the oatmeal. I opened the door of the old
refrigerator and was removing a carton of milk when the
telephone rang.

"Ira? I had somebody in my office before, I'm sorry."

"Sure."

"Hey, I'm glad you called. I've been meaning to get in
touch with you. I hired this chemist guy to work on col-
oring your feather fiber. He isn't doing it right. Can I send
him over to talk to you?"

"Certainly."

"He isn't a moron. He's got a Ph.D. and the whole
thing. But since the feather fiber is your invention, I
thought he could ask you about it and save himself some
time."

"I'd be glad to talk to him," I said. "Send him over.
Any day except today. It's too hot to stay inside. I'm going
out and sit by some water somewhere, in the shade."

"Isn't it ridiculous? I've got my air conditioner turned
down to zero over here, and it isn't doing any good. What
can I do for you, Ira?"

"I hate to tell you. You can do what you've done before. I want to send my daughter a little money."

"Is she still in Paris?"

"Yes."

"Why send it to her? Why not give it to her in person?"

"I don't get it."

"Come with me to Europe. I'm making a trip to sell Feather Fabric to the Scandinavians. I'm leaving tomorrow night from New Bedford. I have my own aircraft now. I don't know if I told you."

"No," I said, "you didn't." I considered his suggestion in a few moments of silence.

"Don't think about it too hard, Ira, just come."

"I don't know whether Henley would be in town. She travels sometimes, with her friends."

"So wire her," Neptune said, "and let me know."

"I might stop in London and see my wife."

"Wire her too," Neptune said. "I have to land at Boscombe Down, in Sussex. You can get a train from there to London. Call me before noon tomorrow."

"Where will you be?"

"Right here, Ira. I'm sorry, three people are standing here trying to tell me things."

"Sure. I'll call you tomorrow."

"Right," Neptune said, and hung up.

I put the receiver back in its cradle. After I had poured the milk on my oatmeal, I put it back in the refrigerator. The milk carton was wet; it had already begun sweating in the short time it had been sitting on the kitchen table. The refrigerator, standing near the entrance to the hallway, was in the darkest part of the room. The kitchen windows would admit morning light but, due to the proximity of the next building, were dark the rest of the day. A steel sink with cabinets below stood against one wall.

There was a kitchen table with three chairs around it and a few dirty dishes on top.

I sat on my bed and ate my oatmeal. Why not go? Portia had invited me earlier. She could have whatever it was out with me now, if she wanted. And it would be lovely to see Henley. I could arrange with the other guards at the school for somebody to pick up my time. They were all my friends, mostly regular teachers.

Somewhere outside, a pile driver started to work. It drowned the humming sound of my electric clock. Between blows, the pile driver's shocks resounded throughout Cambridge, and came back to me as echoes. It was less terrible when I closed the kitchen windows.

I drafted telegrams to Henley and Portia on the back of Henley's envelope. The telegrams to each were essentially the same:

> Neptune wants to take me to London,
> Arriving Fri., 8/26. OK to see you?

With the difference that I added an extra line to Henley's:

> Do you have a telephone?

I called Western Union, dictated the messages, and arranged to have them charged to my telephone bill. Then I left the house, locking the door, and walked down Pearl Street toward Central Square. The pile driver, which was apparently working down by the river, assaulted my back with beats like sledgehammer blows. As I passed a glass-and-aluminum supermarket, a break in the line of three-family wooden houses to my right allowed me an indistinct view of the center of Boston across the

Charles River Bridge. I could see buildings, even their
tops, to a fair distance: the Prudential Tower was blurred
in a white haze, but the State House dome reflected a gold
spot of sunlight.

On the broken brick sidewalk in front of me, a young
man, perhaps a college student, was trying to get a fawn-
colored dog into a Volkswagen. The young man was
wearing plaid shorts and moccasins. "Come here, Buckwheat," he said. But the dog acted as if his mind were
somewhere else.

"Buckwheat, I *said* come *here!*"

The dog persisted in investigating a Mars wrapper on
the sidewalk.

"Buckwheat, could there be something wrong with
your ears? I said *come here.*" And with this, the young man
took the dog by the collar and hustled him into the Volkswagen.

In Central Square, I descended into the subway and
took a train to Boston. I rode on one of those new stain-
less-steel cars that look like they could take a lot of
creative vandalism and still go. On a door at the end of
the car it now said NO ASSING ROUGH. As we passed
over the bridge, I could see the grey concrete MIT buildings marking the Cambridge margin of the river. The
train moved over the bridge at fifty miles an hour, faster
than the vehicular traffic. The river below did its acid
work on the bridge piers and the rocky river banks. There
were sailboats on the river, but their sails hung limp in the
hot haze.

I left the train at Park Street and walked to the Boston
Public Garden, where I passed the afternoon. The swan
boats, with their burdens of little children feeding the
ducks, circulated past me as slowly and yet as out of reach

as any of life's other calm possibilities. Before I returned to Cambridge, I picked up several empty popcorn boxes and a Fanta can and put them in a concrete trash container constructed to look like a tree stump.

T w o

In the night, I awoke in a wave of fear. The feeling was of drowning at great depth under the weight of hundreds of feet of water. Surface swells, bright as if with moonlight, broke above my head. I swam upwards, belted about the chest and pinched in one arm. And broke through, to find Portia's white curtains, illuminated by an outside street lamp, curling before an open window.

Sitting upright, I felt my life returning, but too late to turn back the breathlessness. The pain was coming steadily in my chest, shooting intermittently into my shoulder and left arm. My sighs and gasps alarmed the silence of the kitchen. The electric clock was there, hum-ming from its place on top of the refrigerator and saying it was four-thirty. The white walls and luminous curtains denied shadows and echoes alike as I labored to breathe.

My nitroglycerine tablets were on the floor beside my bed, and I took two of them under my tongue in accordance with Silverman's instructions. I sat up and waited for the medicine to relieve me. My face grew wet with perspiration, and my hands were cold and moist where they rested on the bed sheet. Now that I was upright, my breathing proceeded more evenly. I could see out of the kitchen window into the black space to the left of the adjacent brick building. There were no stars, but the moon was a cold, cleanly shaped ellipse near the horizon.

I am embarrassed that the first impulses these episodes of pain bring me are invariably suicidal. Once, in the early months after my heart attack, I confessed this to Portia. It was evening; she was in the bathtub, and I was sitting on the floor beside the tub. I often watched her bathe after she came home from her workout at the YWCA. Her exercise tights had already been washed out at the sink and were hanging on the shower curtain.

"You want to kill yourself because you're in pain? Half the world is in pain, and they don't kill themselves, they get mad. They rage against it, and they win. They don't give up." She said this as she soaped herself with long, languid motions. Her workout and the heat of her bath had flushed her face and shoulders. Her black hair was piled on top of her head.

"It's because the pain makes me frightened and ashamed."

"Why ashamed? You think the pain is your fault?"

"I feel so embarrassed because I can't do anything about it. I see Silverman and I take his advice, but I don't get better. The pain keeps coming back and it's such a damn embarrassment."

"*It isn't your fault. You aren't your own doctor. Silverman's your doctor.*"

"*I feel the pain, so how can Silverman be the one in the wrong?*"

"*That's ridiculous,*" Portia said. She slid, with an athletic grace, down in the tub to let the water course over her breasts, and I lost her from sight.

When daylight came, I dressed and pulled the blanket up over my bed. I sat in a kitchen chair for two hours between the time the sun came up and the time I knew I could get an answer in Silverman's office. Then I called and asked his secretary for an appointment.

"There are no openings this morning," she said. "I can't do anything at all for you before next week."

"I really have to see him today," I said. "Right now, if that's possible."

"That is *not* possible," his secretary said. "He's at the hospital this morning. Then he has other patients to see here."

"Could I speak to him?"

"I told you, he isn't here."

"I know. I meant, could I reach him at another number?"

"He's in *surgery*. He can't be reached. I'll ask him to call you."

While I waited, I washed out the oatmeal pot. The tap made a groaning sound as I ran the water. It didn't take Silverman long to return my call.

"What's the matter?" he asked.

"I woke up with chest pains the tablets don't stop completely. Also a little dyspnea."

"Didn't that go away when you sat up?"

"Most of it, but I still feel as if I can't catch my breath. My heart is racing."

"You still have pain?"

"Yes."

"Any dizziness or vomiting?"

"No vomiting. Some dizziness."

"I'd better see you. Call Mrs. Marsh and tell her I said to work you in this morning."

I called his secretary again and she said I could come in after ten.

At nine-twenty I called a cab and went out on the porch to wait. Outside, the day was already bright. The wooden porch steps were too hot to sit on. A city work gang had arrived to tear up the pavement in the next block, unimpressed by my emergency. The air above the black pavement and asphalt-shingle roofs was motionless, announcing that the inversion layer above would continue its vaporous oppression another day. The thickness of the air appeared to increase with height, so that the tops of the two trees in the park across from the church waded in a hot cloud.

Silverman's office was on the fifth floor of a brick building to the north of Central Square on Massachusetts Avenue.

"Good morning, Mr. Foxglove," his secretary said when I came in. She indicated the waiting room. It was filled with other patients. I sat down in the only available space on a shaky couch upholstered in red vinyl. Hugo Montenegro had what sounded like every horn and string he could find at work on "Jezebel." All this came out of the tiny speaker of a radio in a white plastic housing.

I waited as the patients went one by one to the doctor. An hour passed, and Hugo wouldn't let up. After we had been through "Hawaiian Wedding Song" and "Night and

Day," an advertisement came along for a feminine de-
odorant spray. By the time the recorded music was ready
to start again, there were only two other patients left in
the waiting room. At the first burst of Andre Kostelanetz,
I reached over and turned the volume down. A heavy lady
who had been reading one of Silverman's *Modern Health*
magazines looked up at me with a startled expression as I
did this. After a minute or two, she got up and left the
room. She returned with Silverman's secretary.

"Did you turn off the radio, Mr. Foxglove?"

"I didn't turn it off, I turned it down," I said.

"Mrs. Randolph would like to have it back the way it
was, please," she said.

I turned the radio back up, and the secretary left.

"I didn't think anybody was listening to it," I said.

Twenty minutes later, I was admitted to a cubicle with
a single window which looked down onto Massachusetts
Avenue. One of Silverman's female assistants took my
temperature, extracted a blood sample from my forearm,
and recorded my electrocardiogram. While she took my
blood pressure with a pneumatic cuff and a stethoscope, I
tried to relax by looking down out of the window at the
hot pavement of the street. The tar flowed under the
wheels of passing heavy trucks, distorting the painted
lines on the crosswalks. The truck tires squeezed the
street, leaving their tread marks behind as if the roadway
were soft flesh.

When Silverman called me I left the cubicle and entered his office. I removed my shirt while he made the
auscultatory examination. He wanted to see my legs, so I
took my trousers off.

"You still have the pain?"

"Yes," I told him.

"The tablets didn't do anything to help you?"

"They helped a little bit, but the pain came back."

"Did it ever go completely away?"

"No."

Silverman put down his stethoscope and sat on the edge of his desk. He picked up a manila folder and opened it.

"I don't see any acute emergency. Your serum enzymes are normal and you don't have any temperature. The EKG is also normal for you. There might be a little S-T elevation, but it isn't consistent. If you were having a frank myocardial infarction, I'd want to see some more signs."

He hopped off his desk and walked around to his chair, where he sat down.

"How's your diet coming?" he asked.

"I'm staying on it," I said.

"Are you?"

"Yes."

"You look heavier today than when I saw you last week."

"I feel heavier today. I always feel heavier with my clothes off when my chest hurts."

Silverman lifted up his glasses and rubbed his eyes, then set his glasses on his nose again.

"I can't help you if you don't stay on your diet," he said calmly.

"But I do."

"How old are you Ira? Forty-five?"

"Forty-two," I told him. He had asked me this lots of times before.

"And what do you eat? Do you stick to that list they gave you in the hospital?"

I always hate to go through this "You are what you eat" stuff with Silverman. It always makes me wonder whether he knows what he's doing. He has this food wheel tacked up on the wall of his office, with all the things you need for a balanced diet.

"I don't eat anything more than the list says. Sometimes I eat less. I substitute oatmeal for things once in a while, but the list says that's O.K."

"You'd do yourself and me a favor if you'd eat what's on the list, no substitutions. Now, how about cigars?"

"How about them?"

"Are you smoking them?"

"No," I told him. Some people absolutely require you to lie to them.

"Good," Silverman said. He rocked in his chair for a moment while we both looked at each other. You can't convince me that one cigar once in a while is worth this prosecuting-attorney routine Silverman does with me. "I think," he began, stretching his arms up and clasping his hands behind his head, "there's a reasonable chance that your angina is developing into status anginosis, which means we're going to have to watch it carefully if we want to keep you out of the hospital. We won't be doing anything new, just the same old routine we had up until now, but you'll have to follow the routine more diligently. That means getting enough rest and exercise, among all the other things. And using the nitroglycerine tablets. You're not still working long hours, are you?"

"No," I told him.

"And how are things otherwise? Are you worrying?"

"What is there to worry about?"

"That kind of talk is cheap," Silverman said. "All my patients worry. They think they're going to die. But they're not. They've got a good doctor."

I stood up and put my trousers back on. I pulled my undershirt down over my head. Silverman was writing in his manila folder.

"I'm thinking about going on a trip to visit my wife and daughter," I said.

"Where are they?"

"My wife is in London and my daughter is in Paris."

"How are you going to go? Fly?"

"Yes."

Silverman rubbed his eyes again.

"Can't you put it off?"

"I can cancel it, but I can't put it off."

"I suppose you really want to go," he said. "That's a silly question. Of course you do."

I didn't answer.

"All right," he said. "Go ahead. It may be just what you need. I'd like to see you get your mind off all this. You can probably help yourself more just now than I can. They have doctors in London and Paris, I suppose. Get yourself to a hospital if the pain increases sharply. It'll be a lot worse than what you had last night if it's serious. It'll feel like somebody put a knife in your chest."

"Oof," I said.

Silverman went on writing in the manila folder.

"Can you prescribe anything for the pain I have now?" I asked him.

"Nope," he said, without looking up.

I waited for him to finish writing. When he put his pencil down, he locked his hands behind his head again.

"I'd like to help you, Ira, but you won't cooperate with me. You won't stick to your diet, you won't do the exercises. I can't give you morphine for the rest of your life.

The nitroglycerine tabs you're taking now have a mild tranquilizer in them to make you feel better. If you need more, take aspirin like everybody else."

I picked up my shirt from the examining table and put it on.

"One last thing, Ira," Silverman said.

"Yes?"

"We'd been discussing the possibility of an internal mammary implant for you, but that's kind of ridiculous under the present circumstances. I'd have to be confident that there was a discrete site of coronary narrowing and that there wasn't much fibrosis in the region of the old infarction. I can't be sure of either with you anymore."

"Check," I said.

"A new angiogram would tell the tale, but as long as you're reasonably comfortable, I'd rather put it off. It's ridiculous to spend two days a week in the hospital having angiograms. So it turns out there isn't much I can do for you. What we really need is a lucky break."

"What do you mean?"

"Well, I have plenty of patients who are as badly off as you are, and nothing I try works, but then their coronaries figure out some way to collateralize and I stop making money off them."

"Tell me how to do that," I said.

"I can't tell you how to do it, it just has to happen to you. Some little artery you'd never know was there just opens up and takes the load around the plugged-up place. You and I have nothing to do with it. We've talked about this before. Don't drive me crazy, Ira. I'm doing everything for you a doctor could do. Go to another doctor if you don't believe me. We can't do anything for a guy with status anginosis. We can watch it and deal with a new infarction, if it comes. Maybe it won't come. Maybe it'll go back to a condition where the nitroglycerine relieves it. Cardiac management gets better all the time. Maybe by next week some whiz kid will have a way to revascularize the whole heart. Better would be to put a plastic pump in. Some day we'll just routinely put an artificial heart in everybody when they reach their fortieth birthday. Not today."

I was dressed and ready to leave.

"Thanks for seeing me when you were busy."

"Thanks for nothing? I wish it didn't have to be. Stop eating candy bars. That much good advice I can give you."

"Now, come on," I said. "That's a load of crap. Give me a little credit for looking after myself. I haven't had a candy bar since I was twelve years old."

"If you say so," Silverman said, smiling. He likes to get a rise out of people once in a while. "See you in two weeks."

A green elevator took me down to the street. Leaving Silverman's air-conditioned lobby was like a physical blow; the noise of the street by itself was a sensible pressure, let alone the light and heat. I walked south on Massachusetts Avenue toward MIT. Signs outside stores selling transistor radios and cheap furniture passed over my head. The entrance of a dry cleaner's shop breathed moist vapors onto the sidewalk. In the display window, made nearly invisible by condensation on the inside of the glass, was a stand-up sign of aluminized cardboard showing a man with a silver face wearing a two-dimensional suit jacket beneath which was printed:

MEN'S SUITS
EXPERTLY DONE

Although the sidewalk and street were heavily littered with papers and occasionally with broken glass, some young people were walking barefoot. A young mother wearing a tee shirt and soiled white shorts supported one child on her hip and led another by the hand. The sidewalk seemed to have been wetted by the atmosphere, but in a way which could never have made it clean.

I called Neptune from the phone booth in the drugstore on the way. He was glad I was accepting his invitation. We would be stopping in Iceland, he said, to refuel and rest. He would take me fishing. Iceland fit so poorly with the phone booth and the traffic noise that I couldn't see it in my mind at all. Nevertheless, I would go and clean up my lab.

Three

I drove to Browning Technical School, an old stone structure surrounded by paved and fenced playgrounds whose basketball backboards formed a vandalized forest all around. The bent and twisted hoops testified to the size of the giants who now attended the school. The building itself rose five floors, each with a high ceiling. The windows of the first two floors were protected with iron grills. The school had been good when I joined it in 1959. It was no longer good; its students no longer wanted to learn. But I was not inclined to leave: I had several devoted friends on the faculty who believed in my after-hours invention work and insulated me from the more unpleasant school chores. Besides, after fourteen years, there were obligations on both sides.

I let myself in and walked the familiar darkened corridor at the end of which I descended a flight of stairs.

My basement workroom was large and had benches against several of the walls. There were only two small windows high up near the ceiling. Machine parts, experimental jigs, and containers of chemicals and adhesives were scattered around. The room was so cluttered with materials and the evidences of incompleted projects that there was scarcely anywhere to stand. I turned on an overhead light and sat down on a daybed placed against one wall. This had been Portia's idea. She and Henley wanted it there for the times they came by to visit me. For four years, when Henley was at the girls' high school in the next block, she'd often sit through the evening with me, doing her homework or practicing on her mandolin while I worked. Portia would sometimes meet us for a late dinner at the Chinese place in Central Square after her gym workout, her swimming practice, or having given a swimming lesson.

One corner of my lab still contains all the heavy spinning and weaving equipment Neptune didn't want when he bought my invention. He took away the old commercial loom I had modified to weave the feather fiber, and he bought all the other equipment from me at the same time but never came back to get it. I have it covered with a white dropcloth to keep the ceiling plaster off but I doubt Neptune even remembers it's here. I'm sometimes tempted to take pieces off it now and then, but I don't because it technically doesn't belong to me. Sometimes I peel the dropcloth back just to look at the stuff. The sight of it brings strong memories of what my life was like when the final success with the feather fiber seemed almost at hand.

Once, when I was at an impasse with its development and I knew I had to discover more about the mechanical properties of biological materials, I attended a conference on medical instrumentation at a Boston hotel. I had paid the registration cost for the meeting, an unusually high thirty-five dollars, out of my own pocket and gave my affiliation as MIT. No one needed to know, and no one asked, that I had stopped short of getting my Ph.D. there.

It was at this conference that I met Alvin Weiss, a professor at the Harvard medical school. He gave a paper on the mechanical properties of skin, and I raised a question about it in the discussion following. After the meeting, Weiss and I discussed his ideas further, and he expressed an interest in my feather fiber project. We exchanged greetings at one other meeting and spoke a few times after that, but that was the extent of our relationship until a year before my heart attack, when Weiss called to say he was beginning a study of a mechanical device to assist a failing heart.

The device was to consist of a rigid sphere containing a flexible bladder, which would withdraw blood from the aorta during the period when the heart was pumping and return it during the period when the heart was filling. The sphere was to be located outside the body on the chest wall, and was to be powered by compressed gas. Weiss asked if I would produce the experimental models for him at my lab and shop facilities here at the school, and he would purchase the materials and equipment needed out of his research funds. I had some previous experience with devices of this kind and doubted several aspects of Weiss's design, including the extracorporeal location. Still, I agreed to make the models.

It only took me about half an hour to put things away in my laboratory. When all the tools were back in their places and the benches were clean, I locked the steel cabinets where I kept my unfinished projects. I checked to see that the FM radio Henley insisted on having down here while she studied was turned off. The floor lamp and an old, frayed armchair next to my desk had also been for her and reminded me that she was far away.

On my way down Pearl Street, I saw Neptune's green camper van already parked outside our house. He was sitting on the steps. He stood up and walked to meet me, grinning, as I came closer. Neptune is several inches shorter than I am, and quite a bit lighter. If I'm average, he's small. He was wearing a wide-brimmed black felt hat with a snakeskin band. Like many of my daughter's young man friends, he wears his shoulder-length hair gathered behind with a rubber band. His jeans were patched with a variety of different types of cloth. He wore a suede vest with long fringes over a blue work shirt.

"Hi, Ira," he said. "What's oscillating?"

We went inside together to get a bag for me. In the kitchen, I gathered up all the pots and dishes, put them in the sink, and ran a lot of water in them. It seemed like a reasonable way of discouraging the roaches. I put some underwear, socks, and some pseudo-clean shirts and trousers into Portia's brown plastic suitcase.

"Did you have to wait long?" I asked him. "I'm sorry I didn't call you. I had to see Silverman and then I went by the school. I didn't really decide to go with you until about an hour ago."

Neptune had walked into the dining room, and was looking at Portia's swimming trophies. "I've only been here about ten minutes. I didn't mind waiting. I like your neighborhood. The people are so friendly."

I was finished packing, so joined him in the dining room.

"Who's friendly?" I asked him.

"A couple of girls walking by. They stopped to talk."

"They probably thought you were selling dope."

"No, they didn't. They didn't ask me for anything. They just wanted to say hello. Don't be so suspicious."

"You're right, I probably am too suspicious."

We walked toward the door. I went into every room and turned out all the lights.

"I think you're missing some opportunities here, Ira," Neptune said. "If I lived in a friendly neighborhood like this with a front porch like yours, I'd get me a classy old rocking chair and sit out there in the evenings. There's a lot twitching around here."

"Do you want to move in?" I asked him as we climbed into his van. "I've got a few rooms I'm not doing anything with."

"That's kind of you, Ira," he said, "but the girl I'm living with now has a six-year-old kid and I don't think she'd go for it."

He started the engine and we drove off. "I'll tell you what I will do, though. I'll get you a nice big chaise lounge for that porch and we'll see if any high school girls want to sit with us on a warm evening."

"It can't be much of a chaise lounge if it's going to avoid blocking the landlady's door," I said.

"What are you being so timid about?" Neptune said. "You look good enough to get these chicks to sit down with you. I'm not talking about fucking them, just fooling with them. Give Portia back a little of her own."

"I doubt Portia would be looking," I said.

Neptune reached the traffic circle under the B.U. Bridge and turned right on Memorial Drive. We passed the Stop and Shop where Portia had been in the habit of buying most of our food, and where I now bought my oatmeal and spaghetti. Farther on was the power station, and then the Harvard houses. Summer school students lay on the grassy river bank by the boathouse in various degrees of nudity. Some were apparently making love while studying.

"How long have you lived in that place, Ira?" Neptune asked me. "You've been there as long as I've known you, haven't you?"

"Yes," I said. "Twelve years. It was in better repair when we moved in. The park across the street was in better shape, too."

"Where did you live before that?"

"Well, Portia and I both grew up in Cambridge, actually in North Cambridge. Her family had bucks, mine didn't. We lived in Charlestown for six years when we were first married."

"*Charles*town?"

"Don't say it like that. It was a nice place to live for that period of our lives. This was before the Mystic River Bridge cast a shadow over the whole place. We lived in three rooms at the top of an old lady's house. You could see the ships coming in and out of the harbor. I got Henley a chart of all the United Nations flags, and she could identify the ships before she learned how to read."

The river, passing by on our left, was bright with glare. There were scullers on the water, but no sailboats here. The oarsmen left swirling puddles which glittered like surfaces of ground glass.

Neptune turned right at the next interchange. This was the end of Memorial Drive. Here, the windows of Mount Auburn Hospital formed a sheer wall facing the river. The afternoon haze was heavy and the air felt soft, but the glass face of the hospital reflected white shapes in the sky behind us which could be clouds. I tried to pick out the window of the coronary ward where I had spent several weeks two years earlier. Why do some people go to one hospital and others to another? I would have preferred the Mass. General, but the ambulance drove me here. Would the result have been any different? Afterwards, Silverman told me I should be pleased to be alive. The anginal pain which remained wasn't life-threatening, he said. Get up, go home, we need the bed. Lose weight, do these exercises, don't excite yourself, take these nitroglycerine tablets under your tongue for pain. See me in two weeks.

I was reasonably comfortable, resting at home under Portia's care, for the next month. Later, on short walks outside, as I held the wire fence circling our house and watched the early spring winds spiraling bits of paper up against the dark mass of the church, the pain had been mild, so that I could be glad to have it and no worse. I could be glad to be free of the unhappiness of the hospital. But every time I climbed stairs, or walked more than a few blocks, or, most humiliating and terrifying of all, each time, in night stillness, I moved my hand from Portia's shoulder to the flannel softness covering her breasts, each time I lifted her nightdress, each time I began the seeking in which we both looked for one another once more, I feared the pain which would come and crush me.

We drove over the Fresh Pond Parkway, past the drive-in movie theater, onto Route 2. Here Neptune speeded up. The sound of the tires became a loud whine. Some fishing poles rattled around under his bed in the back. We climbed the long Belmont Hill in second gear, but were soon moving fast again, with Boston out of sight behind us. For a while, I could tell that Neptune was singing, but the van was making so much noise I couldn't tell what song it was. He kept time by drumming the steering wheel.

By the time we reached the airport, I was feeling worse. The anginal pain which had been flying against my chest all day had lessened, but my ears were ringing and a grey, rancid fatigue overwhelmed me. Neptune drove through an open gate and parked the van beside a rusty hangar building. We got out and opened the side door of the van. Neptune hopped in and handed me our bags, plus four fishing poles and a tackle box. I helped him carry all this into the hangar.

Inside the hangar was a large blimp with the words FEATHER FABRIC spelled out in a giant electric sign on the side. The gas bag, ending in silver fins at the tail, stretched nearly to the roof.

"Is that yours?" I asked Neptune.

"Yep," he said.

There was a small balcony at the rear end of the passenger car. The two engines stood off from either side on pylons. A crew of about ten people were working to move the blimp out of the hangar, guiding it with ropes. A gasoline truck was driving away, apparently finished with the fueling.

"I expected an airplane," I said.

Neptune followed the crew pulling the blimp out of the hangar. "This is better than an airplane," he said. "See that sign? On a clear night, you can read it more than a mile away. That thing really sells for me. All I have to do is drive it around."

"It's marvelous," I said. "Where did you get it?"

"The sign?"

"No, the blimp."

"I bought it used from Goodyear, who made it for the Navy. Since I'm in the rubber business anyway, it's easier for me to maintain it. The price was good. Nobody else wanted it. And having the sign on the side does some things for me with taxes."

"Are we really going across the Atlantic in it?"

"Sure," Neptune said. "I've done it plenty of times. We'll stop in Labrador and Iceland, and we should be in England in three days."

"Who's going to fly it?" I asked. "You?"

"You and I," he said. "I'll teach you. It's easy."

Neptune went off to talk with someone, leaving me to watch the crew moving the blimp out through the hangar doors. As soon as it was clear of the hangar, the afternoon sun made a bright band of reflected light on the airship hull. The gas bag tapered to a stubby point at the nose, where ropes hung down. The ground crew used these ropes to keep the thing from flying away. The whole scene looked like something out of *Our Fighting Coast Guard* or some other such nineteen-forties movie, except for the electric sign on the side.

"What's the matter, Ira?" Neptune said when he returned. "You look like you might be having second thoughts."

"You know I'm game for stuff like this," I told him. "I'm just glad you didn't see a better buy in a PT boat."

We walked under the long shadow of the gas bag and climbed into the passenger cabin through a small door

in the side. I handed the bags and fishing tackle in to
Neptune, and then he helped me up. Once we were in,
the crew fiddled around passing bags of sand ballast out
the door until they were satisfied the weight was right.

The interior was larger than you find in a small airplane. There were three seats on either side of the cabin,
each of the conventional airline-type with safety belts.
The Plexiglas windows were larger than the windows of a
Greyhound bus. Neptune and I sat on opposite sides of
the cockpit. He indicated I should put my seat belt on,
and so I did. He started the engines.

When we took off, the engines roared suddenly and
the ground began falling away at a steep angle. The
ground was several hundred feet below before the nose
came down and we continued our climb more gradually.

Neptune was looking down through the window on
his side. His black felt hat with the horse-tail hanging out
behind obscured his face. The noise of the engines at full
throttle and the pitching motions of the airship as we
passed through the air close to the ground isolated Neptune and me from each other. I looked down at the trees
passing below and was reminded of a time, far in the past,
lying on a bed beside Portia. We were whispering to each
other, looking out of an equivalent window into the air
above a darkened street. Portia was barely seventeen then,
I was eighteen. The apartment belonged to Portia's sister
and her roommate, who had jobs working for an insurance
company. We were sometimes invited to this apartment,
but we were never allowed to be completely alone there.
On this night, Portia's sister and her roommate were having a party in their living room. People kept coming into
this bedroom to stow their coats. If they saw us, they said,
"Ooops, we're sorry," but usually they never noticed us,

because the light was out. We pulled the pile of coats over us to improve our disguise. Portia's bra was unhooked, but I wanted her to keep her sweater on in case the party was over suddenly. The roommate came in one time during the night with a drink in her hand. She had to answer the telephone. The person on the other end spoke for a long time before she said anything.

"You decide what you want," the roommate said. "You get yourself straight and then you come over here. I don't want you to come if you're going to act like you did the last time you were here. Life is just too short."

Portia and I lay very still. My ear was against Portia's chest. My arms were locked around her waist. It would be awkward if the roommate found us. The buttons of Portia's sweater were all open.

"That's fine, that's fine," the roommate said to the person on the other end. "You have my blessing to indulge in those impulses with anybody else but me. Just don't come over here and bother me with your funny ideas."

The conversation, broken with silences for the other party to speak, went on for a long time. Under the coats, Portia's white neck and throat fused into a line of soft skin unbroken to her waist. It seemed like hours that we lay in our warm nest too frightened to move, and I listened to the beating of Portia's heart.

As we climbed up through the lower levels, the view from the windows showed the ground as a green, rolling plain beneath an atmosphere of steam. The haze, contaminated by pollutants from below, muted the details of the towns and cities and rivers. Occasionally the sun's reflection from a lake or a single window in a house marked a bright point. We passed over the white beaches of the coast of southern New Hampshire, and then only the ocean flowed below. As we leveled off, the engines became quieter and changed their note. The cabin stopped shaking and it became possible to talk again.

Neptune released his belt and came across the aisle to sit in the chair behind me.

"How do you feel?" he asked me.

"Fine."

I had to turn around and raise my voice a little. The earlier pitching motion of the airship seemed to have stopped, for which I was grateful. The cooler air was making me feel better than I had on the ground.

"What exactly did the doctor tell you today?"

"He said he couldn't do anything for me at the moment. I think the implication was that he couldn't do anything for me while I was still alive."

"Why take that shit from him? Get another doctor. I'll stand you the cost."

"I owe you too much as it is."

"Baloney. I'll get an appointment for you with somebody really good when we get back."

"Silverman's perfectly good," I said. "I don't doubt he's doing the best he can for me. In fact, I keep having this dream where I'm pedaling a swan boat in the Public Garden and Silverman's on the dock, jumping up and down and waving his arms. He wants me to come back so he can take my place. He scolds me for taking a chance with my heart, exercising in the hot sun. Then he takes the boat out himself, and I watch him from the shore, pedaling the children across the water."

Neptune listened to all this with his chin resting on the back of my chair, smiling.

"Do you think he's really like that, Ira?"

"In my dreams he is. He seems to really care what happens to me in my dreams."

"O.K.," Neptune said, "Right. Anyway, the offer still stands. Let's see what's on our dinner menu." He brought out a black lunch box that had been on the floor with the tackle boxes and rods.

"Shucks," he said. "No oysters and champagne."

"I can't eat them anyway."

"Can you eat a meatloaf sandwich?"

"I think so," I said. "If I really loved Silverman, I'd look it up on my list."

"Why don't you just eat it," Neptune said, "seeing as it's all we have here. Do you want some lemonade too?"

I took half a meatloaf sandwich and a small cup of lemonade. They were excellent. When we finished the sandwiches, Neptune found hard-boiled eggs and Mounds bars in the bottom of the lunch pail. I passed up my Mounds bar, so Neptune ate both of them.

"Who makes your meatloaf sandwiches?" I asked.

"Mickey," Neptune said. "That's the girl I'm living with now. She made this vest, too."

"Pretty nice," I said.

"She is pretty nice," Neptune said. "I like her little boy, too, although sometimes things are strained there. He misses his father. But it's something we work on a lot together, because Mickey and I are thinking of getting married."

"That's great," I said. "Good luck."

"We're not thinking about it too hard because we were both married before and it didn't work out."

"That doesn't mean there's anything wrong with you," I said.

Neptune was silent for a moment. "You're fantastic, Ira. I wish I could be so peaceful with myself."

I watched him put the Mounds wrappers and wax paper away in the lunch pail and close the lid.

"You really think I'm peaceful?" I asked him.

He looked at me. "I think you're serious, and you have troubles. But you seem to be working away on your troubles all the time. They don't make you do crazy things."

"They make me think about doing crazy things."

"But you don't. That's what counts."

"All this reminds me of one conversation or another I've had with my wife."

"How so?"

"She used to say that I was surprisingly faithful."

"To her?"

"To her, to my school, my friends, and maybe even my illness."

"Wow. That's a lot to fault you for. You mean she thought you didn't want to get over being sick?"

"I think so. But remember that Portia spent her entire childhood as a shut-in, a polio cripple. And she put all that behind her, very much mind over matter. She worked her way out of her handicap completely, all except for a little limp she still has when she's tired. She did it with that fanatical swimming."

"I haven't heard you call it fanatical before," Neptune said. "But I think you're right, it is."

"Of course it is."

Neptune sat back in his chair and looked out at the ocean. It was getting darker.

"Still and all," he said, "You must have been sympathetic to that swimming bit at one time. It's such a big part of her."

"Oh, I've never stopped. It's fascinating. It lights her up. Before she started it, she was just this little cripple girl, from what I gather. By the time I met her, when she was seventeen, there was nothing crippled about her at all."

"How did you meet her?"

"I haven't told you this before? She was giving swimming lessons at the M.D.C. pool and I was her student. There were about five other people in the class, all adults. I was the only one close to her age. At the beginning, she used to stand waist-deep in the pool and hold us up while we practiced our kicks. I was crazy about her from the moment I saw her. I became the star pupil. I went to the pool every time I had a few hours, even when I knew she wouldn't be here. After a while, she was making me an example to the class at nearly every lesson. I went to all her swim meets, even the ones out of town. She encouraged me to think about being a competitor, and we spent a lot of time together."

"Then you asked her to marry you?"

"Yes. When we were married, she still had two years to go at Sargent College. After Henley was born, Portia went through some depression. She wanted to swim and the baby wasn't letting her. For most of the first year, I was the one who took care of the baby. Portia minded her during the morning, but then I would take over, after classes, and Portia would go out. This went on for a long time and pretty soon Henley wasn't a baby any more. Then I could talk to her as well as take care of her. We talked her whole childhood away."

The sun was disappearing under a sediment of clouds above the coastline to the west of our course. Straight down the black water was scratched by incandescent lines: whitecaps. I looked out at the engines and the fish-scale discs of the propellers. The long hull above the cabin reflected the sun's red glare.

Following Neptune's instructions, I got the hammock out of a locker in the passenger cabin. It was designed to swing between sets of steel rings located fore and aft on the cabin bulkheads. I made the passenger seats on one side of the cabin recline all the way to give the hammock more room. I took off my shoes and made myself comfortable in it, covering myself with blankets from the locker. It was lovely to be up in the cool air. Life seemed to have a better prospect here than in the heavy heat of Boston's clouds.

"Do you want me to wake you up when we get to Goose Bay?" Neptune shouted back to me. "We should be there sometime before dawn. It's just a refueling stop. I'd sleep through it if I were you. There isn't much to see."

"I'd like to see it," I said, "If you don't mind calling me."

"Not at all."

From where I swung in my hammock, I could see only about half of Neptune, his face and right arm illuminated by the red of the instrument panel. His felt hat was lying on the seat I had been in earlier.

"I wonder if I could possibly have things figured out right," I said.

"You want me to tell you? I doubt if I can."

"Portia and I disagree, you see. Fundamentally. According to her, I function by weighing myself with obligations. I have obligations to my school, to my daughter, to you, to Silverman. I owe money all over the place. Portia thinks I do this on purpose. I jail myself so that I can jail her. We'll die in jail together."

"I don't know, Ira," Neptune said. "I don't think you're going to die, but I doubt you'll get your wife back, either. Somehow you'll have to do neither."

"We'll see about that," I said.

Four

We reached Goose Bay in the early morning hours. I opened my eyes when Neptune woke me, but I never got around to climbing out of the hammock. The refueling and resupplying took only an hour. We were in flight again shortly after the sun rose. I remember passing over fishing vessels at low altitude as we climbed away from the coast.

When I awoke again, my watch said ten o'clock. The cabin was bright with sunlight. On the walls were framed photographs I hadn't noticed the previous evening. The photographs were of historical events involving airships. In these pictures, men swarmed like pests under the giant shapes of dirigibles being taken out of their hangars. The

legend in one photograph said that the view below was
Count Zeppelin's erection barn near Freidrickshafen.
Count Zeppelin himself was in another picture. But the
one that held my attention showed a simple, amorphous
cigar-shaped bag underhung by a small carriage. The indistinct head of a single man was visible in the carriage.
The balloon was suspended in an ashen, glare-ridden sky
over a grey sea: a hawser hung down at a steep angle to the
surface of the water. The photograph had apparently been
taken from the deck of a ship. It carried the handwritten
title at the bottom:

> Airship *America* rescued at sea
> By the Steamer *Trent*, Oct. 18, 1910

Outside, glacial clouds stood on the northern horizon.
Although we were flying at only a modest altitude, I felt
cold enough to wrap myself tighter in the blanket. The
ocean swells below were deep blue this morning. Details
of the surface of the water, scuffed by winds, were visible
through a mile of transparent air. I have a poor opinion of
the ocean, generally: it's brackish and undrinkable, in
contrast to inland bodies of water, which are fresh. This
seems like an inversion of what ought to be the natural
situation. After all, the larger the volume of air you con-
sider, the cleaner it gets.

The sight of the ocean put me in mind of a week we
spent on the Maine coast when Henley was six. The cottage, which belonged to a school colleague of mine, was
close enough to the rocky shore of a bay for Portia to swim
there in the late evenings without a bathing suit. I remembered the cottage itself as small and dark. Portia had

been having a troubled week, with some stiffness in her legs. Henley had been uncooperative. Once, on a trip to the grocery store in the town, Henley had refused to leave the store without a Dreamsicle. She and Portia had engaged in a verbal battle, ending with Portia's attempt to pull her by one hand from the store. They went through an enormous scene in the doorway of the grocery, and a group of people gathered around disapprovingly. Someone in a self-righteous carload of teenagers pitched a watermelon rind which struck Portia's back. Catcalls taunted her to pick on someone her own size. Henley shrieked all the way home.

Later in that week, Portia left the cottage as usual for her evening swim after Henley had been put to bed. I was reading a book by a lady author with three names entitled *Just Call Me Happy* under a feeble light in the main room off the kitchen. The story, narrated by a golden retriever puppy, took you through the trials of one year's farm life for a family straight from the city who had inherited rural property. In this year, the golden retriever puppy grew up amidst breezy winds of fortune. One of the little barn kittens had just been lost down a well when I looked up at the clock and noticed that Portia had been gone an hour longer than her customary time.

I waited for another half hour with a growing sense of alarm. Checking to see that Henley was still asleep, I left the cottage and walked to the beach, where there was still no Portia, only her bathrobe dropped on a branch. I borrowed a neighbor's outboard motorboat and set out to find her. The night was clear enough to see every detail of the surface of the water, but the path of reflected moonlight made a confusing, moving highway, with blackness at its shoulders. I knew her approximate route and steered toward a tiny island, which was in reality a lone rock sticking up out of the center of the bay.

As I came closer to the rock, I saw Portia sitting on a ledge just above the water. She pretended not to see me. I cut the motor and called her name. Still no response. I landed the boat on a sloping part of the rock fifty yards away and tied its bow rope to a scraggly tree. Beer cans among the weeds showed that this was a well-known romantic spot. I made my way toward the ledge where Portia was sitting, and spoke to her again just before I reached her. When I was almost upon her, Portia gave me the finger and slid into the water. She dove under the surface, and I lost her from sight until she reappeared again, far out, swimming in the direction of another small rock island. I took off my clothes and dove into the water after her. She hadn't taught me to swim for nothing. In a short time, we were together on the other island, our chests heaving from the exercise.

"You swim pretty well, Ira," she said, "for somebody who sits around all the time. You should practice more. I always thought you could be good."

We kissed. Her arms and back reflected the moonlight like a naked steel penknife blade. We coupled like athletes.

I got out of my hammock and sat in the copilot's chair beside Neptune again. He was glad to see me.

He looked at his watch. "You slept nine hours."

"Wow," I said. "that's about twice as long as usual. I feel much better. This has been a good change of air."

"Put your feet up on the rudder pedals, there."

"Why?"

"I'm going to teach you how to fly this thing," he said. And so he did. I learned how to make the nose swoop slowly from side to side with the rudder. He showed me how to climb and descend using the throttles on the instrument panel and the elevator wheel beside our seats. It all seemed quite simple. When I was younger, I had taken flying lessons in small airplanes, and had even flown solo several times. Neptune's blimp was easier to fly than an airplane—things happened so much more slowly. Neptune gave me a heading to hold on the compass, and then left me alone while he stretched his legs. Ten minutes later, I looked back to see where he was and was surprised to find him curled up in the hammock. Master of the airship, I cruised us on our course eastward for over two hours before Neptune came forward again. He heated us coffee over an electric hotplate. As we drank the coffee and ate blueberry muffins, the western coast of Greenland came into view.

"We're here," Neptune said. "This is the spot."

He went back into the passenger compartment and untangled his fishing equipment.

"Take it down, Ira," he called. "I'll tell you when to level off."

I pulled the throttles back a ways and put the nose down. The ocean drifted up closer. At my back, I heard the door in the rear of the cabin open. I turned to see Neptune ducking down to step out on the balcony, which was open to the elements except for a railing circling its edge. Neptune moved an aluminum camp chair out there, opened it, and then came forward to speak to me.

"Those chairs aren't the safest," he said, leaning over my shoulder. "I have to hook my foot around the railing

while I'm holding my pole so I won't go over if I get a really big strike. You can level it off now."

By this time, the blimp was down to within fifty feet
of the surface of the water. The coastal shoreline of
Greenland, still miles distant, appeared to sink into the
ocean as we descended. Below, no whitecaps were in evi-
dence. The engines slowed, we turned into the light wind,
and the blimp came to a stop, hovering barely thirty feet
over the water.

He baited his hook and dropped it over the side. After
about ten minutes of hauling the line up and down and
peeking at the surface of the water for his bobber, Neptune looked over at me.

"Are you warm enough?" he asked. "There's a blanket
just inside the door if you want to wrap yourself in it."

"I'm just barely warm enough," I said. "If you'll please
catch a fish quickly."

"I'll see what I can do," he said. "This is a tremendous
place. I've had a lot of luck here before."

"The old fishing hole," I said.

"What?" Neptune cupped his ear toward me.

"Nothing," I said. "Skip it!"

In the distance, the coast of Greenland was just a line
of rocks. I supposed there were mountains of ice farther
inland, but they weren't visible from our low altitude.
Neptune's line hung down into the water in a graceful
catenary like the hawser from the airship *America*. I
wondered what would become of us if we ran out of fuel
or if the engines failed. Airplanes crash when that happens, but I guess blimps just float away and are never
heard from again.

Ten minutes later, Neptune came forward again.

"They aren't biting?" I asked him.

"Right," he said. "They aren't biting. Look, Ira, your teeth are chattering. You should put on one of those jackets I have here."

"I like it. It's healing me. There isn't any haze or smog up here. And I can see so far."

"You aren't bored? People who ride with me in this thing complain that it takes too long to get anywhere."

"Not in the least," I said. "I'm fascinated."

Neptune reeled in his line with a great whirring flourish. His hook broke the surface of the green depths to the left of our shadow. The bobber, with the hook trailing behind, fiddled up through the air to the balcony.

"I wish the frigging fish were fascinated," Neptune said. He wrapped the line around his pole and secured the hook on the reel.

"Don't you want to stay here and catch some?" I asked him. "Don't stop because of me."

"I'm not," he said. "I'm stopping because of that."

He pointed to a steeply rising front of black clouds on the western horizon.

"We'd better get going before those bastards catch up with us," he said. "The fishing's better in Iceland, anyway."

Five

We were still climbing a half hour later when we passed over the western coast of Greenland. Flying inland, we found desolate tundra cracked by hundreds of tiny fresh streams. The ice and snow I had visualized never appeared; we were apparently too far south. Before reaching the eastern coast, we passed over some bald, craggy highlands at close range and frightened a group of deer-like animals grazing. Neither Neptune nor I knew what sort of creatures these were, nor whether they were wild or tame.

When we joined the ocean again, the storm clouds which had been chasing us across Greenland were now hours behind, but another front, certainly part of the same system, deviled us from the north. These clouds had tops which ended in icy anvils, and they were occasionally lit by lightning. Neptune didn't seem worried, but he decided to stop over in Reykjavik until the weather cleared, rather than try to fly through any of those squall lines.

We reached the coast of Iceland four hours later and were soon slanting down toward the American military-built airport at Reykjavik. Showers were falling in isolated spots around the airport as we approached, and yet the sky directly above was not even overcast. Although my watch said it was ten o'clock in the evening in Boston, the sun in Iceland was only halfway to the horizon. Rainbows curved in the air to the south of the airport over the ocean as rain fell through spaces where the oblique sunlight could find it. The land near the coast was covered with green grass, but a short distance inland the grass stopped and a grey-green carpet of lichen began.

I was interested in watching the landing operation, which I had missed at Goose Bay. Neptune let down ropes that had been coiled on winches near the nose of the gas bag during flight. A crew of about fifteen people were waiting on the ground in the form of a V to receive us. Neptune flew us down slowly toward these people, passing over their heads at a height of no more than twenty feet. The airship was moving at a walking speed at this moment. The people grabbed the ropes and hauled us the rest of the way down to earth. Once the single wheel under the passenger cabin was down, we opened the cabin door and brought enough ballast aboard to keep us from floating up again. The landing crew then walked us to a slender mooring post guyed upright by wires. The nose of the airship was made fast and we disembarked, the crew adding ballast for each passenger removed.

After we cleared customs in the commercial airline terminal, Neptune and I loaded his fishing gear and the army jackets, plus extra blankets, into an old green Volkswagen.

We drove away from the airport through a suburban part of Reykjavik. I was struck by the fact I hadn't seen any trees growing in Iceland, and yet there were many houses built of wood. I asked Neptune about this and he said he supposed they shipped it in from Scandinavia.

Leaving the outskirts of Reykjavik, we drove down long straight roads through the lichen bogs. Crops of volcanic stone and fields of low yellow flowers provided occasional relief from the grey-green plane of lichen. Farther on, we climbed over hilly country where the grass reappeared, and herds of sheep. The roads we were driving on, which had been unpaved since we left Reykjavik, jarred us with long washboard stretches. Fields next to some of the farmhouses appeared to be planted with wooden stakes. Neptune told me that wires were strung between these stakes for the purpose of hanging herring out to dry. We were still close to the ocean. I saw gravel beaches several times, once as we passed through a fishing village.

Neptune bashed his head on the roof of the car when we went over a particularly bad pothole. After that, he wore his felt hat, and tried to avoid potholes.

"I hate to whack my head like that," he said. "I'm always afraid that some day I'll be tapping my head absentmindedly with a ruler or something and poke through a soft spot."

"Only babies have soft spots," I said.

"Are you sure? Mine feels a little weak right here on top."

We stopped in a village to eat and had an excellent meal of flounder and Danish beer. By the time we were outside again, a steady rain had begun to fall. I noticed large birds with lustrous black plumage sitting on nearby roofs.

"Pretty fat crows," I remarked.

"They're not crows," Neptune said, "They're ravens."

For the next hour, we worked our way over a poor coastal road which was all but washed away in several stretches. Neptune turned on the headlights, and the resulting feeble bouncing light on the road ahead of us had the effect of magnifying the apparent size of the rocks and ruts. When we reached our destination, an ancient Danish inn built on the side of a hill near the town, the rain was particularly heavy. It was for every practical purpose night, even though a pale light filtered down over the courtyard of the inn. The midnight sun was evidently still there, somewhere behind the clouds. Neptune and I took a large room together, and I was asleep almost immediately.

The following morning, we arose too late to have breakfast with the innkeeper, a fisherman who owned a small trawling vessel. Neptune was disappointed, because he wanted me to meet this man, who had become his friend on an earlier visit. We had our herring, bread, and coffee at an old table spread with a checked tablecloth in the nearly dark dining room. The walls of this room were stone, as was nearly the entire inn. The only bright lights, which came through the door leading to the kitchen, made our water glasses flash when the door was opened.

Back in our room, we dressed warmly. Neptune put on a sheepskin vest under his army jacket, and offered me a wool shirt to go under mine. His wool shirt was tight on me, but I found I could wear it by leaving the front unbuttoned. Outside, we found the rain still lightly falling.

The Volkswagen balked at first, but finally started. Neptune had taken a pair of rubber wading boots out of his bag, and put these in the back seat of the car with our fishing gear. We were going after freshwater salmon in a mountain stream only a few miles from the inn. As we were loading up, I looked up at the peaks of the inn roof and saw several ravens perching soundlessly there in the rain.

When we reached the river, we found it surrounded by thick bushes. Neptune said he couldn't remember those bushes having been there before, and we spent a fruitless twenty minutes trying to get into the river before I suggested that we drive further and look for a clearer place. We got back in the car and Neptune tried to start it. Nothing. It wouldn't start. The starter motor would turn it over, but the engine wouldn't start. Neptune rested his forehead on the steering wheel and looked miserable.

"What a place for this thing to crap out," he said. "What do you think is the matter with it?"

"It could be wet," I told him, "although I doubt it, because it started this morning."

I noticed a raven sitting in a nearby tree watching us. The rain was making less noise on the roof of the car now: it was letting up.

"I wish I knew something about machinery," Neptune said. "I just go on hunches. That's why we're sitting in this old fucked-up car right now, because I believed in it. This will kill you, but I brought this car all the way from Cambridge because I drove it there for ten years and it never broke down. I thought because it never broke down before, it never would."

I got out and opened the engine compartment. The fuel pump was soaked with gasoline.

"Do you have any tools?" I asked Neptune.

"Not any good car-type tools," he said, "because I was convinced this thing was a perpetual motion machine. I have some Mickey Mouse tools in my fishing box."

I found an adjustable wrench and a screwdriver in his fishing box.

"I really envy you, Ira," he said, sitting down beside me in the mud behind the car. "You just took one look at the engine and you know how to fix it."

"It isn't running yet," I said.

"But it will be, because you know what you're doing. You know how to fix things, and no one can tell you you're wrong. Take it from somebody who knows, that's better than depending on luck."

The little adjustable wrench was just barely satisfactory to get the fuel pump off. Once it was out of the car, I gripped it between my knees in order to use both hands on the screwdriver. Removing the screws holding the two halves together was a long job because they were on so tightly. Neptune took out his harmonica and played while he watched me. After a while, he stopped.

"I'd like to know what those obnoxious ravens find so interesting," he said, jumping up. He picked up a stone, and, running toward the tree, threw it. Several black birds flew away into the dark rain clouds.

"This fishing trip is working out about as well as my first marriage," he said when he came back.

He sat down on the bumper. "Getting married was just one of the things I did the year after I flunked out of Cornell. That was ten years ago. When I knew for sure that I was booted out, I called my mother in New York, who called my father in Singapore. He was out at some rubber plantation, and nobody knew how to reach him. A few days later, he got the news and cabled me to stay where I was. He flew straight from Singapore to Ithaca and bunked with me at my fraternity house for a few days until we finished our plans."

"Your plans or his plans?"

"Oh, Ira, come on. What's the difference? I didn't care. *I* didn't know what to do. He had a lot of friends in business in Los Angeles, so we went there. We stayed in a motel for a week, and every day we went to see one of his friends, looking for a job for me. I couldn't get back into school for a year, so I had to have a job. In the evenings, we sat on the bed and watched television. We both drank all the time, and he said terrible things about my mother. Finally the job offers came through. I picked one. Then he bought a car for me to get to work in and went back to Singapore."

"This really doesn't explain how you got married."

"Yes, it does. I stayed at that same motel and worked at my job for five months. They taught me how to program a computer. I did that all day, and then I came back to the motel and watched television. I had to drive thirty miles on the freeway every day, and I'll tell you, I was scared to death. Have you ever been on a California freeway? You're sandwiched in between these trailer trucks and Cadillacs going eighty miles an hour, and you can't even see what's in front of you or behind you. I had this little MG my father bought for me, and I never knew whether I was going to be squashed the next moment. I had to drive at rush hour to get to work on time, and I almost had an accident every day. The freeway was on my mind all the time. I went to the Red Cross and gave blood about as often as they'd let me. It was ridiculous to think I could keep their blood bank filled up all by myself, but I wanted to do what I could to make sure they had enough when my accident came. I saw it in my dreams: the glass all over the road and my MG under the rear wheels of a Trailways bus."

"Sorry to interrupt the story," I said, "but how about holding this part of the diaphragm while I stretch the other side?" I had found a split in the diaphragm of the fuel pump, but fortunately it was going to be possible to stretch what remained of the good part to fit over the hole. Neptune held the diaphragm taut while I tightened the screws.

"Thinking about it now, I suppose there were other things about Los Angeles I didn't like, but the freeway managed to be the symbol for everything that was threatening me. Driving to work one morning, I passed a terrible wreck. Somebody's Chevrolet was half on one side of the road and half on the other. The traffic was moving slowly past, driving over the broken suitcases and dolls. They were putting the people into ambulances, and I wanted to shout to them, 'You go on to the hospital. I'll be there later. I'm giving blood this afternoon.' I was so shaken that I had to turn around and go back to the motel. I was going to wait there until the rush hour was over and make another try at getting to work, but instead, I found myself packing. I left the MG in the motel parking lot and took a cab to the airport. That evening, I was back in Ithaca, living at my old fraternity. They let me eat with them and party with them, and for a while I was happy. I thought about trying to get back in school early, but I knew it would be impossible. After one of the parties, I went to bed with a girl who would only tell me her first name, Claude. We stayed in my room for two days and talked and fucked the whole time. There was a fake red leather sofa with broken legs in that room, and we sat on it with our arms around each other and looked at old copies of the *National Geographic*. We found these lovely pictures of the Rocky Mountains. They were fantastic. Beautiful flowers, dark rocks with blue sky behind, mountain waterfalls, and wild cherries that we planned to eat when we got there. I wanted us to get married before we started, and Claude agreed. I sold a ring my father had given me, and we paid our bill at the fraternity. We caught a ride with one of the brothers to Ohio."

I had the fuel pump together again and was ready to put it back in the car.

"Do you want me to stop talking so you can think about what you're doing?" he asked me.

"Certainly not," I said. "I can listen and work at the same time. Keep going."

"I'm almost through, anyway," Neptune said. "After that, we rode on our thumbs. Most of the time, I let Claude stand out in the road to get the rides. She was a good sport about it. She had to stand there with her thumb out, wearing about as little as we thought she could get away with, no matter what the weather was. When the ride stopped, I'd come out from behind a tree or signpost and she'd say, 'Is it O.K. if we take my husband too?' That worked so well that we had all the rides we wanted. Money was another matter. I looked for little one-day jobs wherever we stopped, but I didn't make much. Claude and I started having arguments about money and other stupid things like would we or would we not have sex in a cornfield. She called me a lot of names, first jokingly and then seriously. Whenever we'd be sitting in a diner, she'd say 'Hi' to the truckers who came in because she found out it made me mad. She also teased me by saying that if she really wanted to get away from me, she could just forget about letting me in the car the next time she stopped us a ride. As it worked out, she never had the guts to do that. She called her parents, and they sent her money to come home. We got the marriage annulled, and I never saw her again."

I had nearly finished the job. Good thing: Neptune and I were both completely soaked. My hands were raw from working in the cold rain.

"Did you really mean you were thinking of getting married again?" I asked.

"Not right away," Neptune said. "I still have a bad taste in my mouth from the first marriage episode."

"Do those things eat meat?" Neptune pointed out the ravens, who had come back and were now perched in a nearby tree watching us.

"Don't worry about that," I said. "Go and try to start it. You'll have to let it crank for a half minute or so to work the air out."

The engine started. Neptune let out a whoop. He jumped out of the driver's seat and ran up and embraced me.

"That was beautiful, Ira," he said. "It was beautiful, and it was something I never could have done in a million years."

"It wasn't any big thing," I said. "There never was any real danger. We could have walked back to the inn in an hour or so if I hadn't been able to get it going."

"It *was* a big thing," Neptune said. "We were stuck here, and you knew what was the matter and fixed it. There aren't many people who can depend on themselves like that."

We drove farther on, to a place where the river came close to the road, and there Neptune waded up and down along the bank, fishing in the cold rain. He never caught anything. After our bread-and-cheese lunch, I felt pleased

with myself, for no good reason, and lit up a stogy. Silverman be damned.

The next morning was clear. We packed the Volkswagen under the stares of the ravens and began our trip
back to Reykjavik. Neptune was disappointed about the
fishing and said very little as we bounced along. With
the air dry and the sun warm, it was possible to see more
of the landscape. The mountainous inland terrain was
made of a purple volcanic rock. Stretches of the road we
drove over, paved with gravel made of pulverized rock,
were sharp enough to cut the tires.

We stopped and had a late breakfast midway on our
trip. After that, Neptune's mood improved. He brought
out his Icelandic fishing license and unfolded it to show
to me. It was as big as a map, printed in three colors, and
signed by two cabinet ministers. I folded it back up afterwards, but it took me three tries to get it right. Neptune
put it in the tackle box with a sigh.

The blimp was ready to go when we arrived. Once we
were aboard, the crew came and guided us out with the
ropes again. Neptune said only a few of these people were
employees, the rest were local volunteers. They launched
us and then stood around waving goodbye as we climbed
up into the cool air. We turned and flew out over the blue
Atlantic. I watched from my seat for a while, then covered
myself with a blanket to let a few hours go by.

Toward noon, I went out on the rear balcony to
stretch my legs. There was a chemical toilet aboard, but
Neptune preferred to pee over the railing into space. I did
the same. We passed over a larger tanker and saw several
small fishing boats. The noise of the propellers in cruising

flight was so deafening that we didn't stay out on the balcony long.

The coast of Ireland appeared in mid-afternoon, and by evening we were passing over Wales, then Bristol at the mouth of the Severn, and at last the Salisbury plain. We landed at the flying field at Boscombe Down, where, as in Labrador and Iceland, Neptune maintained a mooring mast. We slept in a bed-and-breakfast establishment near the airport. The next morning, Neptune called a cab to take me to the railway station in Salisbury, and we waited for it together on the sidewalk outside the hotel. While we were waiting for the cab, Neptune gave me a wad of cash in English and French currencies.

"Look," I said, "I don't know how much there is here, but it looks like more than I could pay you back."

"You'll pay me back," Neptune said. "Sooner or later, you'll finish this heart thing you're working on now and we'll both make a fortune on it."

"I don't think we can count on that."

"You just finish it," Neptune said. "Then we'll see. Your inventions are subtle enough so they sometimes do things you never thought they were going to do. Like feather fiber."

"There's always a sense in which they manage to be unsatisfactory, though. My inventions."

"They earn you money."

"O.K. A little bit. But in every case, even the ones I've sold, the problem wasn't really solved. There was always enough finished for me to be able to leave it, but never as much as I'd hoped."

"All of which leads me to wonder what you hoped."

"I wanted them to work, that's all."

"They do. Feather Fabric works. People love it."

"People buy it, but they don't need it."

"Who says they don't need it? We get letters all the time from young ladies who say it changed their lives."

"It didn't do what I designed it to do."

"So what? It does a lot of other things."

The cab came and we put my bag in. Neptune was smoking a cigar; he clamped it between his teeth in order to be able to use two hands on my bag as he put it in the cab.

"See you back here in five days, then," he said. We shook hands, but I didn't answer. I got in the cab.

"Somehow you don't look like a tourist, Ira," he said through the window.

"But I am."

"Where's your camera?"

"I don't need one. I remember everything."

"You're a spy, then."

"I guess I'm a spy," I said. "But I'm not taking any trouble to hide myself. People know I'm coming, I mean."

"Have a good time," Neptune said. "Don't worry about a thing."

"See you soon," I said, and the cab pulled away.

S i x

The English countryside, seen from the train, was alarmingly beautiful. We passed through shallow dark green valleys, which may have contained rivers, although I never saw any. I stayed awake in my seat, although others around me slept. It was one in the afternoon when the train reached Waterloo Station. In the covered bay where the trains stopped, light fell down from high windows and illuminated the diesel exhausts, turning them a light yellow color. I left the coach and walked alongside the train. Steam escaping from fittings in the couplings between the cars curled out into the air. There was a translucent canopy high above. I carried my bag past a baggage platform and a newspaper dealer. I found a taxi stand through some glass doors.

I gave Portia's address to the cabbie who picked me up. He was a small white-haired man in a frayed purple sweater.

"Near King's Cross, isn't it?" he asked me.

"Beats me," I said. "I've never been here before."

We went grinding off in first gear, and were soon in the thick of fast-moving traffic. The cabbie drove very quickly, even through crowds. He threatened people off the road at intersections. The iron fences which were apparently there to prevent people from jaywalking weren't entirely effective. Stone buildings, some newly cleaned, others darkened by soot from an earlier, coal-fire age, marked the edges of the street. In the central shopping district, we turned left into a series of narrowing streets, where traffic forced the cab to move more slowly. The iron points of a fence around Russell Square cast short shadows, which people had to step in as they walked by. In Portia's neighborhood, signs advertising coin laundries and small shops hung over the sidewalk. There were Indian restaurants and old hotels adjacent to vacant lots. Were these WWII bomb sites? Many of the people on the sidewalks here were dark-skinned.

Portia's address was one blue door of many in a three-story brick structure. I paid the cabbie and took my bag up the three steps to the door, which I found open. Inside, there was an entranceway with several mailboxes on one wall. Among them, I found one marked Dawlish Warren, which was the name Portia's friend used in business. All my mail to Portia had to be sent in care of this fictitious person Dawlish Warren, because he conducted all his transactions under this name, believing that his Hindu name was too complicated for English people.

Before me, a flight of darkened stairs rose up through a windowless hall. I heard the sounds of children coming from the upper floors. I started to climb the stairs but met another person on the first landing, coming down. It was Portia.

"Hey," she said. "What are you doing here?"

"I came to see you."

"Ah."

"I sent you a telegram. Didn't you get it?"

"I got it but I didn't think you meant it."

"I did mean it."

Portia's black hair was longer than it had been in Boston. Her shape was still excellent, as always. She was wearing a blue cotton blouse and a red plastic miniskirt. A naked bulb on the landing above her spread light down in such a way that part of her face was dark, but the part that was lighted was full of contrasts.

"I was going out to the food store," she said.

"I'll go with you. If you'll just point out your door so I can use your bathroom first."

"The bathroom is all the way down the stairs on the left."

I galloped down the stairs, found another short flight under the first and a door leading to a bathroom at the bottom. I latched the door from the inside and used the toilet, which was in disagreeable condition. I washed my hands and face in the washbasin, but this turned out to be a little overzealous because there were no towels available. I dried my face with my handkerchief. And then wondered whether I had really spoken to Portia. Could it have been someone else?

She wasn't on the landing when I returned, or in the hall. I climbed the stairs to the second floor, but that hall was empty and all the doors were closed. I called her name once, but there was no answer. The closed doors lined up like a basketball team while somebody is making a foul shot or whatever.

I returned to the first floor and called for her again. Still silence. Where?

My chest hurt mightily. Portia had eluded me again. There seemed nothing left but to go back to the bathroom and flush myself down the toilet.

But then Portia opened the front door, flooding the place with outdoor light. Her shape was a silhouette against so much light. "I'm out here," she said.

In the food store, Portia took a wicker basket at the door and carried it on her arm up and down the narrow aisles. I followed her. She bought cottage cheese and several very small cans of tomato paste. At the meat counter, she bought a shoulder of lamb. I kept amazing myself by looking away at the fruit stand and then looking back to see that Portia was actually there. On the last of her orbits through the aisles, I let her go alone. She moved slowly, stopping with her hand on her hip to look at things on the counters, bending over sometimes, looking at the labels. The backs of her knees, even at such a distance and with so many people passing between us, looked the way I remembered them. As she went around the counters, I lost her from view for a few moments, but by shifting over one aisle I was able to find her again, coming toward me. When she reached down and pulled out a sack of potatoes, I rushed over to help her with it.

"They're having a good deal on oranges," I said, grunting as I heaved the sack up under my arm. "Two for a penny."

"What?" Portia said. "Where's that?"

"Right over here," I said, and I showed her.

"That says two *shillings* and a penny. This little slash mark here separates the shillings from the pennies."

"Oh," I said. "I didn't know that."

Portia unloaded her wicker basket on the counter in front of the cashier. The cashier added everything up, and she paid him out of her wallet. It was the same old wallet Henley had made for her in a school crafts class. She had a string bag in her purse, which she brought out and helped the cashier fill up with her groceries.

When we were out on the street again, I suggested that we stop somewhere and have a cup of coffee. Portia agreed, but said that she wanted to get back to her place early enough to wash her hair before dinner. We walked west until we came to the Kingsway, and found a small restaurant above an expensive-looking toy store.

The stairs leading up to the restaurant were covered with a red carpet held in place by brass bars. The wallpaper in the stairwell was also ornate, apparently hand-painted: a bird of paradise stretched his wings from the first floor landing to the top of the stairs. We were shown into a room with cream-colored walls. From there you could see into the main dining room, where a long table set with silver and crystal appeared to be awaiting a dinner party.

Our room had several windows looking down on the Kingsway, and one of these was open at the top, but we heard no street noise. We were seated at a table to one side of the room. I helped Portia with her chair and then sat down opposite her. When the waitress came, we ordered tea. After the waitress left, we were the only people in the room.

"You know, I've just thought of something," I said.

"What?"

"I should have known you were about to leave me when you started sleeping with that pillow between your knees."

"Nonsense," Portia said. "I just do that to keep from bruising my knees. I was doing it long before I left. I still do it here, even."

The waitress brought our tea. A young man and a lady took the table behind us. The young man, who was a bit fat, wore a three-piece suit. His lady friend was dressed somewhat like Portia, but used a lot more makeup. They immediately began speaking in tones loud enough for us to overhear. The girl was talking about someone she met on the train coming to London. After the waitress took their order, she changed the subject.

"You'll be proud of me," she said. "I informed John by post that I was coming to London to see you, and that I expected to see you directly on getting in."

"How *marvelous* of you."

"I knew you'd say that."

"He still writes you, then, does he?"

"He writes me notes. Some of them have demands. The last one demanded to see me alone, my place, eight o'clock prompt."

"Really. Demanded to see you alone. What did you do about that?"

"I wasn't there. I went with Anne to the cinema."

The waitress brought their tea. No one said anything for the time it took to unload the tea tray and put the milk and sugar in. They had toast and cakes with theirs, as we did with ours.

"That was naughty of you. Not to keep your appointment."

"It was no appointment of *mine*. I didn't say I'd meet him. He proposes to me regularly, you know. It's so boring."

A silence here, with stirring and clinking noises.

"Ever think of taking him up on it?"

"Not really. I don't like him that much. What do you think of him?"

"He's sort of *cold*."

Portia, across the table from me, took a slice of toast from the small silver rack. She tore it in half and spread raspberry jam on one piece. I loved the way she lifted her lips out of the way as she bit into it. I wondered if she was listening to the people behind us.

"You like warm people, don't you?" the girl was saying.

"Yes, I do. Very much."

"Well, that's not John. He was very bothered, you know, extremely *upset* that time you tried to kiss him on the lips. We talked about it a great deal. He was terribly threatened by that. Did I tell you?"

"No," the man said. "You didn't." He said this in a kind of sleepy, snoring voice.

"Well, he was. I told him you didn't mean anything by it. I said of course you were just joking around. You didn't mean anything by it, did you?"

"When was this? Michaelmas, wasn't it?"

"Yes, that was it. You were just joking, weren't you?"

"I can't remember. Perhaps."

Portia pushed the toast and jam pot toward me. "Try some," she said. She was looking after me again, like old times. If I took the jam pot from her, the tips of our fingers might meet. But no.

"I can't," I said. "Silverman would make every bite poison. He thinks I'm killing myself with snacks."

"How are your parents?" the girl at the table behind us asked.

"Very well. They knew I was seeing you today, and they asked to be remembered to you."

"They *adore* each other, don't they?"

"Yes, I believe they do."

"I think it's wonderful when two people reach their age and still have so much love for each other. I know they love you very much, too. It must be a great comfort for you to feel their love."

"Yes, it is," the man said.

"I made my dad and mum hate me. I wore pink lipstick and all the makeup I could get on my face. You should have seen them flinch. And tight clothes. I wore tight, tight clothes, the tightest I could find. That's when I was just a silly little virgin. Do you remember me as a virgin?"

"Um. Yes," he said.

"What were you like as a virgin? Not like me, I suppose. Do you remember yourself when you were a virgin?"

"Actually, no."

"I suppose you got rid of your virginity long before I did. When did you? I was still flitting around in my tight little virgin's costume when I was seventeen."

"I was fifteen."

"Was it a boy or a girl?"

"A boy, actually."

Portia had finished her tea and was ready to go. I motioned to the waitress for our check. She brought it, and I put the money, plus a tip, on her silver plate.

"Life is too complicated for words," the girl said. "I always thought it would be wonderful to get married and have love from someone all the time. I wanted a baby and a pram. Everyone I knew did. Now that I'm old enough to have those things I don't want them, but I don't know what I want instead."

Portia and I collected our groceries from the spot where we had left them under the coat rack. We walked down the plush staircase and were out on the street before either of us said anything.

"I thought that was going to be a quiet place, but it turned out to be Grand Central Station," I said.

"What are you talking about?"

"The people behind us. The beauty and the beast."

"She wasn't such a beauty," Portia said.

"She had beautiful expectations. Did you hear what they were saying?"

"A few words. Not much."

"Oh. I thought you were listening."

"I wasn't," Portia said.

This kind of cocky behavior might have got Portia pushed into a closet in an earlier time of our lives. I used to be able to bully her into a sexual mood on occasions when tenderness was out of the question. She's still the most physical person I've ever met in my life. I changed the subject.

"Your aunt sent a bunch of stamps for Henley last month. She thinks she's still collecting."

"She is."

"But her stamp books are all at home."

"She has some new French ones. I saw them."

"Well, then," I said. "Maybe I'd better send her Jane's stamp packet. There seemed to be some good ones there, although I'm no judge, of course. I'm surprised that Henley's still doing it."

"Why?" Portia asked me.

"I don't know. She's all grown up now. I thought stamp collecting would be kid stuff to her."

"She isn't all grown up," Portia said. "She's only eighteen. She still likes the things she's always liked."

We caught a big red bus and rode it for five blocks. We sat together on the double seat near the stairway. I liked the way the lady conductor takes your money with one hand and cranks the ticket thing around her waist with the other while standing with feet wide apart as the bus jolts ahead. We got off in Portia's neighborhood, only a few doors from her apartment.

As we passed the letterboxes, Portia checked under Dawlish Warren to see if there was any mail. Dawlish Warren. Portia said he didn't come home until after six o'clock, and the time was still mid-afternoon. She went up the stairs before me. I followed her heels, which moved rhythmically as if she were treading water. The plastic mini bounced with each step. As she turned the corner at the landing, her breasts swayed to the outside of the turn a little. We reached the second floor, and I followed her down the hall to a scratched brown door. She put her string bag of groceries down, and, reaching into her blouse, brought out a set of keys that were tied around her neck. When she had the right one, she bent over until the key fit in the lock and let us into the apartment.

The inside of the apartment was dark, even though this was a bright day. Portia turned on the light. It was really just one big room, with a cooking space in an alcove. I noticed, with a sense of rising expectation, that there was no double bed to be seen, only two single beds on opposite walls. A large wardrobe took up most of the wall adjacent to the single window, which looked out into a broad alley. Through the window, I could see that someone had strung several clotheslines between hooks worked into the brick walls of the two buildings defining the alley.

Portia put the groceries on a junky wooden table near the middle of the room. I put the sack of potatoes beside the groceries. The next thing Portia did was to open the window, but in order to do this she had to move a bicycle with a Solex motor attached to the front wheel out of the way. I helped her park it against the wall with the wardrobe.

"This thing doesn't work," Portia said, as we moved it. "I wish Dawlish would either get it fixed or throw it away. It's been sitting around here all winter."

"What's wrong with it?"

"I don't know," Portia said. "The motor doesn't start."

I sat down on the one bed that was made up while Portia put away the groceries on shelves above the small gas stove.

"How long can you stay?" Portia asked me with her back turned.

"No fixed time," I said. "I have to meet Neptune to go back in five days. I wanted to spend a little time with Henley while I'm here. But otherwise, no real plans."

"You can stay here with us if you don't mind sleeping on the floor. We can borrow a mattress from upstairs."

"That sounds fine," I said.

Portia's long back stretched as she reached up to put things away on the top shelves. I was reminded of the steel cabinets over the sink in our Pearl Street place. Portia would come in through the front door, carrying groceries down the hall, into the yellow kitchen. I would be lying on the couch in the parlor, because this would be just after my heart attack, and I would be worried about dying. Portia would put the food away without even greeting me.

The sounds of the cups going away in the steel cabinet are harsh and unsympathetic. I feel Portia's restlessness. Nothing seems to promise any relief, least of all the chest pain. The pain is a statement of my account.

"What can I do to help?" I asked. "Can I help take care of those dishes in the sink?"

"Oh, thanks just the same, Ira," she said. "I'm not going to do them now. I think I'd better go on up to the tub on the floor above us while it's quiet and wash my hair. I've been putting it off for a week."

"Can I sweep or something while you do that?"

"No, there really isn't any housework to do here, it's so small. Neither of us are here much. I'm usually in the pool all afternoon."

She unbuttoned her blouse and took it off, hanging it on a hanger in the wardrobe. The miniskirt had its own plastic hanger with clips to hold it. Portia modestly turned her back and removed her bra, a low-cut black one I hadn't seen before, and put on a terrycloth robe, all in one motion. Then she stepped out of her panties and tied the terrycloth belt around her waist.

"Are those paper underpants?" I asked.

"Yes."

"I knew it. I knew you'd want to try some of those when you came here. How do they work?"

"Fine," Portia said.

"You just wear them a couple of times and then throw them away, right? It sounds like a great idea especially if you don't have a washing machine, which I guess you don't. They don't feel too scratchy or anything?"

"They're not scratchy at all."

"I'll have to try some," I said.

Portia took down a towel and a bottle of shampoo from a shelf in the top of the wardrobe. She put on her slippers, which were under her bed, the one I was sitting on. She did this by stepping into each slipper, then lifting each foot and pulling the heel on. As she stood beside me, I reached up and took one of her hands and pressed it against my cheek. And held it there for a long minute.

She sat down on the bed and slowly, slowly leaned her head on my shoulder. Her breast touched my arm through the terrycloth bathrobe.

"Ira, why did you come?"

"To see you. I still *love* you."

"Did you hope to bring me home?"

"I always hope that."

"You shouldn't. I'm not ready to come back yet."

Seven

While Portia was in her bath, I washed the dishes in the sink. I used a green dishwashing liquid that made a snorting sound when I squirted it into the sink. I enjoyed putting my hands in the warm water, which came out of a small electric hot-water tank connected to the tap. When I was finished, and the dishes were stacked on the draining rack, I found a broom in a closet and began sweeping the floor. It wasn't very dirty. Portia came back while I was sweeping, to put away her shampoo and pick up her electric hair dryer.

"I usually use it upstairs in the bathroom where we don't have to pay for the electricity," she said. "Do you mind? I'll be back as soon as I can."

"That's fine with me," I said. She took her clothes with her as she left.

When I was through sweeping, there was the problem, again, of how to occupy myself until Portia returned. I rolled the motorbike out into the room, pulled a chair over, and had a look at it. Since there wasn't any starter cord, it was obvious that the motor was supposed to be started by engaging the friction drive arrangement with the front wheel while the bicycle was being pedaled. I lifted the front wheel and jerked it to pull the motor through. It wouldn't start. I started checking things. There was fuel in the tank and the fuel tap was turned on. I took the spark plug out with a wrench I found under the seat: it looked clean. There was a cap covering the points. I took it off, using the screwdriver on my keychain, and found the problem. The points were corroded and pitted. I cleaned them up with the blade of my screwdriver and was about to put the cap back on when the door opened.

A dark-skinned man wearing a summer suit came in. "Who might you be?" he asked me.

"I might be almost anybody," I said, "but actually, I'm Portia's husband."

Dawlish closed the door behind him and came over to where I was working. "What are you doing?"

"I'm fixing your motorbike," I said.

He watched me while I put the cap back over the points and screwed the spark plug in.

"Why?" he asked.

"Why not?" I answered. "I don't like things to stay broken." I tightened the spark plug and put the wrench back in his toolkit. "Let's try it now and see if it works. Lift up that handlebar so that the front wheel is off the ground."

He did as I asked. I lifted the other handlebar, engaged the motor, and gave the wheel a pull. It started immediately, making a *suckahaha, suckahaha* sound which gradually built into a lawnmowerish buzz.

"How do you turn it off?" I shouted.

He pressed a button on the handlebars and the motor cut. The inertia of the front wheel kept it spinning after the motor was silent. The wheel stopped when we put it down on the floor. I pushed the bike back into its corner just as Portia opened the door.

"Wow," she said. "It smells like a garage in here."

"We were just trying out his bike," I said.

"Did you fix it?"

"Yes," I said.

"What was wrong with it?" Portia was now wearing a light blue sleeveless dress. Her hair was clean and beautifully brushed.

"The points were dirty," I said.

Portia put her hair dryer away in the wardrobe. "Well, no wonder," she said. "Have you two been introduced?"

Dawlish was silent. "We figured out who the other one was," I said.

Portia's face showed disapproval. She went into the kitchen alcove, where she reached up for a bottle of sherry and three glasses. "That's not very friendly, Ira," she said. "This isn't going to work if you're not friendly."

I instantly felt ashamed and embarrassed. She was right: I was their guest, I should take it easy on the spleen.

"Sorry," I said. "I didn't mean to be rude. Dawlish just came in. We haven't had time to say hello."

Portia poured us all a glass of sherry, then excused herself to begin preparing our supper in the kitchen. Dawlish took off his shoes and invited me to take mine off too.

"The English people won't take off their shoes unless they ask everybody first. I know I should ask everybody, but I forgot," he said.

"You don't care," Portia said.

"Why should I ask here and here and here if I can remove my shoes in my own flat? I don't understand that." Dawlish put his feet up on the edge of the bed near his chair. "Where are your cigarettes?"

"In my purse."

"Where is your purse?"

"On the doorknob."

He got up and fished through Portia's purse for her cigarettes. He found one, lit it, and returned to his chair. I made myself useful by setting the table with plates, glasses, and silverware from the dish drainer.

"Sit down, Ira," Dawlish said. "My mother would be crazy if you did that in our house. The men are never allowed in the kitchen." He smiled. "It would also make her crazy to see me smoking this damn cigarette. Smoking and drinking, too. I never did these damn things before I came to this country."

"Your mother doesn't like you to smoke?" I asked him.

"Oh-ho, I'll say she doesn't," Dawlish said. "Not smoking, or drinking, or any of the rest of it. If she saw me, she would punish me very well, I'll tell you. Me or any of my brothers. We were never allowed to do these things." He drew deeply on his cigarette, making it crackle. "But here I drink, and here I smoke, and here I have girlfriends, because all those forbidden things are only in the culture and it's different here." His words took shape as filaments and eddies of smoke. "It's very different here. At home, we are taught how to keep from poisoning ourselves and we are taught how to bear the troubles that god gives us. But here, you do what you damn well please and then you weep and curse god when the evils come. Isn't it true you weep yourself to sleep?"

"Doesn't everyone?"

"I know not everyone does. I want to know if you do."

"Me personally?"

"Of course."

"I did, sometimes. When I was very sick."

"You wept and pitied yourself in front of your wife, she told me this."

I turned to Portia, who was standing at the stove.

"You told him that?"

"Why shouldn't I?" Portia said. "It's part of what happened."

"It didn't happen to *him*!"

"This is a very stupid conversation," she said.

A silence prevailed while Portia spooned out the vegetables onto our plates. Each person got some boiled spinach, canned corn, and a potato.

No one spoke for the rest of the meal.

When we were finished eating, Portia suggested that we go out and have a drink somewhere instead of sitting glowering at each other. We walked out into the dusky twilight, closing the blue door behind us. The air on the street was soft. The evening was beginning to be cool. Cars and taxis passed us at great speed with only their parking lamps on, no headlights. The sky was a lighter color toward the brightness of the theater district. We got in a cab and Dawlish gave the driver an address in Piccadilly.

Our destination turned out to be an acid-rock bar called The Jerked Beef. You had to go down a flight of concrete steps to get to the door of this place. Inside, we pushed our way through a jam of people dancing and rubbing against one another. Three black musicians backed up a white girl singer on a low stage near the bar. We waited, pressed against a wall, for a table to be free. Everywhere around us, young Londoners in striking clothes danced, or talked, or drank. Dawlish made his way to the bar and left Portia and me alone for a moment.

"I'm not trying to antagonize him, he just doesn't want to be friendly," I told her.

"Let's just make the best of a bad situation," Portia said. She spoke nearly into my ear, because of the loud music. "I wasn't sure you were coming so I didn't say anything to him. He doesn't know what you're going to do. He feels threatened."

"For Christ's sake," I said.

"What?"

"I said for Christ's sake. Why should *he* feel threatened? He's holding all the cards."

"He's worried," Portia said. "I can tell. You don't know him yet. Don't dismiss him before you see what he's like. He's a real person. He cares what happens to other people. He's been very kind to me. So just be careful."

Dawlish found a table and motioned for us to come over. He had already bought a pint for himself and me and a lager for Portia. We had some difficulty sitting down because the other chairs crowded in on us.

"There you are," he said, pushing my pint towards me. "English beer. Have you had it before?"

I told him I hadn't.

"Drink it slowly," he said. "It's stronger than American beer."

I liked it. "It's very nice," I said.

"You see that, Portia? Your husband likes his pint already. We'll make an Englishman of him before he goes home."

On all sides, the dancers bucked about, boys and girls in turnover-neck jerseys, tailored jackets, miniskirts, mesh stockings, half-bras, white leather vests. They spawned in great fluid currents. Colored spotlights changed the girl singer's flesh from white to emerald green.

"How many Hindus do you see here?" Dawlish asked. I looked around. The faces were all young and English.

"None," he said. "You won't see a single one here. They wouldn't come in such a place. I wouldn't either, when I first came to this country. But now here I am, and I bring other girlfriends here too, not just Portia. I eat meat, I drink beer, just like an Englishman. I even use the laundrette."

"What's sinful about laundrettes?" I asked him.

"My mum told me strictly not to use them," Dawlish said. "They're not clean. She wanted me to do up my own clothes. I did that when I first came. I washed my things in my sink. I put up a line outside between the two walls. That was hard, I'll tell you. I had to pick, pick, pick between the bricks to put my pegs in. Then they were always falling out. If the sun came out in the middle of the day, I would take a tube back to my flat and put my washing out, then rush back to work. I've stopped saying prayers in the morning. I no longer bathe each day. And now I even use the laundrette. It's no good to be religious here. When I go home to my family, I'll be a good man again. Here it's not possible."

"I wouldn't say you were such a bad man," Portia said.

"Because I made a place for you. But I would always do that. It's fundamental to help those without a house to stay in. Your money was gone, and you hadn't anywhere to sleep. We would always do that for another person. But it doesn't make me a good man. Here is your husband, and he wants you back with him. I shouldn't be his rival."

"Don't worry about it," I said.

"You aren't his rival," Portia said, "You're his friend. You're taking care of me. He knows that."

"Why don't you go back with him? I thought it was because he doesn't sleep with you. But there must be more. I don't understand. It makes me sad."

The young London working class jigged about us. The lights on the singer changed color with each new phrase of her song. She cupped the steel stalk of the microphone with her fingertips. Her nails, where they caught the light, were iridescent. Her breasts, heaving under the sequin dress, shook like refrigerator desserts.

We had another round of beer just before leaving. While Dawlish and I were arguing at the bar about who would pay, a young man in a double-breasted suit asked Portia to dance. He coughed smoke in her face while making the invitation.

"Sod off," she told him. We drank our beer and watched the dancers without saying much to each other.

By the time we got back to their flat, I was unbearably tired. The rancid taste of illness and fatigue had returned to my mouth. Dawlish and I went upstairs to borrow a mattress from a friend of his, and I nearly dropped my end on the way down. My mattress was put in the middle of the room between the two single beds. The night was clear, making the room quite cool even though we shut the windows before going to bed. I was restless and found myself sleeping and waking by turns all through the night. I happened to be awake when Portia crept out of her bed and spread an extra blanket over me sometime before the cold dawn.

Eight

I was awake before the others the next morning. As soon as I had my clothes on, it was plain I should leave. A dull overcast had spread over the sky, keeping the dawn light faint and subdued. I put my belongings in my bag and folded up the bedclothes. In my pocket was Portia's watch, a present I had given her before we were married. She had left it behind, perhaps because the watchband was broken. I had been meaning to fix it, but since it's Swiss, I'd been having difficulty getting a part I needed. Now I brought it out and put it on the kitchen table. I found a pencil in a cup. On the back of one of my checking deposit slips, which I don't find much use for, I wrote:

I shouldn't hang around here while I'm
acting so mean. I don't really feel all
that wronged, certainly not by you people.
Let me spend a little time with Henley, and
I'll drop in on my way back and take you out
for a meal, hopefully in a better frame of
mind. I'll get your watchband fixed, too.

                                              —Ira

I closed their door behind me as quietly as I could and
went down the stairs. As soon as I was out on the street in
the raw, damp quiet, I regretted my note. "Wronged." It
sounded so self-pitying. They hadn't said anything particularly apologetic to me while I had been there; apparently
they weren't blaming themselves for my troubles. So my
note would work as an accusation. People don't like to be
accused. I thought for a moment about going back. I could
get rid of the note and pretend I had only gone for a walk.
It was Saturday. We might all go to the British Museum or
something, and spend the afternoon in a pub. I could sit
beside Portia on a red leather bench while Dawlish, in a
chair opposite us, told us about his homeland. Perhaps
there'd be a fire on the hearth in this pub: the day was
cold enough for it.

But no. I needed to leave. I really didn't feel like being
peaceful with Dawlish. A cab came by and I hailed it.

"What's a good way to get to Paris?"

"Why you can fly, sir, or go by boat. I think I'd fly, if I
were an American."

"Good. That's what I am. Take me to the airport."

"Do you have your ticket, sir?"

"No."

"Then I'll take you to the air *terminal*, sir. You can get your ticket there and take an excellent bus out to the airport. If I drove you, it would be very dear indeed. Even for an American."

At that hour of the morning, the traffic through London was very light. When the first dots of rain appeared on the windshield, we were passing Regent's Park. It was green and empty except for a man in a Sherlock Holmes hat holding a limp leash. His dog was investigating the foot of a park bench. The white globes on posts marking pedestrian crossings blinked but very few pedestrians were there to take advantage of them. Regent's Park, with its ornate iron fence and planes of green, reminded me of the Boston Public Garden. And for a moment the memory of swan boats embarrassed me. They weren't out of place at home, but they would be so undignified here.

At the air terminal, I bought a ticket at the BEA counter that would get me to Paris at ten forty-five. I sent a short telegram to Henley, since I still didn't have her telephone number, telling her when I would get in but urging her not to bother meeting me at the airport. The bus connecting with my flight didn't leave for half an hour, so I sat down in the terminal coffee shop for a little breakfast. I was the only customer.

"I almost didn't get here this morning," the serving lady said when she brought me my fish and toast. The fish had a boiled tomato lying on one side of it. The tomato was soft and flaccid, like an uncooked organ, perhaps a heart. "We live in Brixton, and my husband drives me here. This morning, one of our tires went flat. My husband has a bad back, so I had to jack the car up and change the tire myself."

I could see why this might have been difficult for her. She was a heavy woman, maybe in her fifties.

"I suppose they have push-button jacks in America," she said, pouring my coffee.

"Not that I know of," I told her. "But don't take my word for it. Life gets easier all the time."

"Right you are, sir," she said. "Right you are."

My Viscount landed at La Bourget in a light rain near mid-morning. The flight across the channel had been in the clouds nearly all the way, with only a rare glimpse of the ocean near the coast of France. I passed through customs easily. On the other side of the customs barrier, waiting among a group of other people meeting the flight, I spotted Henley. She returned my wave. I made my way through the crowd and put my bag down by her feet.

She put her arms around me. "Daddy," she said.

She kissed the front of my shirt. She's shorter than Portia and me. I used to think that maybe she was going to spurt up, but now that she's eighteen, I suppose she's finished growing. The top of her head comes to my chin, which makes her about five feet five. I hugged her and kissed her temple. Her hair is black, like Portia's. It was clean and beautiful. She was dressed in rodeo clothes: a denim shirt and blue jeans.

"You weren't supposed to meet me," I said.

"I wanted to. Besides, it was necessary. You would have gone for a twenty-dollar taxi ride otherwise. It's part of their welcoming ritual."

"No, I wouldn't," I said. "I was planning to pass for a Parisian."

"Fat chance," she said. She put her arm around my waist as we walked toward the exit.

"Well, who does pass for a Parisian these days?" I gave her denim shirt a little tug. "Jane Fonda?"

"Come on, Daddy," she said. "What you don't know is that this is high-fashion stuff. It costs a fortune if you buy it over here. I'm lucky I brought mine with me."

"I wish I'd known. I would have worn my old white sneakers."

We put my bags in a cab. Henley told him where we wanted to go in what sounded like perfectly good French.

The back seat was upholstered in an interesting red velvet material. Once we were moving, Henley took my hand. I looked down at her slim wrist. It had a simple silver bracelet on it. I stroked the downy fuzz on the back of her arm with a tentative index finger.

"You look wonderful," I said, "but thinner."

"You're thinner too, Daddy."

"Ah. So my scales tell me. But this doctor I'm seeing accuses me of being overweight every time I go to see him. I wish you'd tell him that I look thinner."

"I think a lot of people are being more careful what they eat, now," Henley said. "Just on general principles. My instructor at the school is always telling us how to feed ourselves. Eating and elimination are big things to him."

We were soon away from the airport and traveling on a wide concrete highway in the midst of trucks and buses. I asked Henley more about her school, and offered a regret that she had to miss it today to come and pick me up. I shouldn't worry, she said. They were practicing a production, but she had only a minor part which wouldn't be rehearsed until the afternoon session.

"Did you stop in London to see Mother?" she asked.

I told her I had, and in fact I had spent the previous night there on someone's borrowed mattress.

"Was the mattress grey with cigarette holes burned in it all over?"

"Yes."

"I wonder if it was the same one they got for me. Probably was."

"When did you visit them?" I asked her.

"Last month. Her friend Dawlish seemed awfully nervous about me. He must have been afraid I was going to stay."

"It was a little bit the same way with me," I said.

"He wasn't what I expected," Henley told me. "From what Mother had written me about him, I expected him to be a lot more spiritual."

"Oh, I don't think he's spiritual," I said.

"No, he isn't. He keeps telling you he knows better, but he goes on acting gross anyway. He says England corrupted him. I don't know why it corrupted him, it doesn't seem to corrupt anybody else. And he acts like he's doing Mother such a favor by letting her stay there."

"I noticed that too," I said.

"When I was there, they were talking about whether or not she should pay him rent. Do you know if she pays him rent now?"

"I couldn't say."

"Well, I think he's a big disappointment," Henley volunteered, releasing my hand. "And if you ask me, Mother's got her head up her ass."

We drove through the outskirts of Paris into increasingly congested traffic. Although my flight from London hadn't taken me over any great distance, the climate seemed to have suffered a marked change. The buildings in these broad streets slapped back the noise of street construction and traffic. The city haze lying in layers above the streets and green places seemed to propagate the sound all the more harshly. Drivers criticized each other through the open windows. We left our taxi hopelessly mired in traffic on the Boulevard St. Michel; Henley paid the driver with one of my colorful French banknotes. While we had lunch at an outdoor café, Henley spread my coins and bills on the steel table and explained how much each was worth.

After our wine and cheese lunch, we walked down the Boulevard St. Michel and crossed a bridge. The Seine flowed under our feet and carried tourists on sightseeing boats, floating paper cups, and used prophylactics. I thought I saw their white mouths languidly opening and closing. The people walking across the bridge were almost all young, dressed as I was used to seeing students dress in Harvard Square. Many wore packs on their backs, often bearing the flags of their home nations. We overheard English spoken more often then French, but there were also many Japanese.

"I like this part of town," Henley said.

We stopped on the bridge and looked down into the water for a while.

"There are a lot of young people here," I said.

"Well, it's August, so of course all the French are gone, but even during the year, there are a lot of nationalities here, many students. Old people too, though. They live in those houses."

Henley pointed vaguely along the river banks where dark stone buildings rose and fell until the river turned and flowed under bridges lost from view.

"Come on, you don't really mean old people live here, do you?" I asked her.

"They're here," she said. "They come and sit on the benches, all alone. They feed the birds."

"Old people are always alone," I said. "It's just one of those great things that happens after a while. All the people you know and love manage to work themselves out of the picture one way or another. Then there you are with your bag of birdseed."

"Daddy," Henley said, putting her arm through mine and threading our fingers together. "You're not old."

"That's what I keep telling myself."

"Well, you should believe yourself. You're O.K."

Below the bridge, around its piers, the unsteady surface of the water flowed, sometimes catching the sun's reflections in its oily planes. By this time I was getting ready to admit that the used safes were probably not that at all but bits of white candy wrappers or some other childish refuse. There were just too many of them to be the other things, even in Paris.

"Let's see," I said to Henley cautiously, "I've got a problem here because I don't want to give this moment completely over to self-pity, it's so disgusting, but on the other hand I need to know what you think about your mother quitting me and all, because on the one hand it's such a big puzzle, and on the other I suppose I know why she did it."

Henley kept holding my hand. Maybe she tightened her fingers a little. "Why do you think she did it?"

"Oh, I think it had a lot to do with my getting sick. I just kind of lay there like a corpse for about a year afterwards."

"That doesn't seem like a very good reason."

"Well, maybe I gave her the creeps. I suppose it wouldn't be very nice to live with someone who spends most of the time playing dead. Especially for Portia, because she has all these strong childhood memories of nearly getting snuffed out by polio, and all. It was probably much harder on her than me, although I'll admit I was quite alarmed myself."

Henley released my hand and leaned with both elbows on the bridge railing. Her hair fell forward. She smoothed it back with one hand. "Still," she said, "it was shitty of her."

As our silence grew longer, I knew that my daughter didn't have any new information for me. She hadn't been any further into Portia's labyrinth than I had. In fact, it looked as if I probably knew more than she did, and given that that were true, I shouldn't take her down any deeper.

Henley shifted her weight to one foot and sampled the texture of the bridge railing with a scraping motion of her index finger. "I wouldn't presume to give you advice," she said, "but if it were me, I'd be tempted to write old Mommy off."

"I can't," I said.

The school of mime was in the top floor of an old building made of stones that may have been white once but were now the color of a tidal flat when the water has gone out. The stairs that brought us up to the third floor supported us with steel treads, as if we might have been leather-booted roustabouts. The building was apparently a converted warehouse. Heavy fire doors at the top of the stairs opened into a single room that occupied the entire top floor. Just under the roof beams, high translucent windows let in the light which fell down on a rough wooden floor, covered in several spots by padded gym mats sewn together into practice areas many yards square. An office took up part of one wall, and a stage including a curtain was against another. In front of the stage were random nests of folding chairs, and above these, suspended from beams in the ceiling, were powerful arc lamps. There were rooms for dressing and other private matters, informally constructed of fiberboard walls. Stage props and stacks of more folding chairs leaned against these walls.

Henley's classmates were rehearsing their production on the stage. It was hard to decide whether or not they were in costume, but I finally judged that what they were wearing, costume or not, also served them as street clothes. The young lady on the stage had apparently fashioned her top out of two men's handkerchiefs and a few skimpy pieces of gift-wrapping twine. The two men with her under the hot glare of the arc lights wore no tops at all. All three were in faded blue jeans like Henley's, but through a split in one of the men's pants it was possible to verify that he wore no undershorts.

The work was an original script of theirs, an adaptation of St. Joan to mime. Henley said, as we sat down in a pair of folding chairs away from the stage, that they were well behind where they should have been by this time in the afternoon. Considering that this was supposed to be a silent craft, there seemed to be a lot of talking going on.

"Who's the guy in the blue sleeveless tee shirt?" I asked Henley.

"That's Henri. He runs the place when Michel isn't here."

"He's doing a lot of shouting."

"Yeah, he's a turd."

We watched for a while. It took me some time to catch on to the action, which seemed to convey that Joan and her lieutenants had reached Orleans, and were preparing to dispatch instructions to their troops for the attack. Every few minutes Henri would lose his temper with the young woman's performance and run up on the stage to show her how to do it.

"Why is he picking on her?"

"It's part of his dreary technique," Henley whispered. "If he fancies someone, he shouts at them all day in rehearsal, and then afterwards he takes them to dinner at his place and plucks them like a shivering flower to show his criticism isn't personal. In fact it's quite the opposite, he only rages because he's serious about you as an artist. The ironic thing about all this today is that Peaches Piluski is so bad that she really deserves to get shouted at. She knows it, though, so it isn't as pathetic as it could be."

"What did you say her name was?"

"Peaches. She's an American. She lives with us in the Annex. You'll meet her later."

In the next scene, Joan was reunited with her troops. Henley left me sitting alone to take her part in the chorus of soldiers who joyously lifted Joan onto their shoulders. After carrying her around for a time, they set her in the lap of one of the male students who was sitting in a crouched position, evidently representing some kind of honored chair. Then several of the soldiers, including Henley, each acted out a report of what they had seen in their various liaison trips to the city that was to be besieged. As well as I could understand it, Henley's report had to do with going by boat into the enemy garrison and impersonating the wife of a military commander. Henley's dramatization of moving over the water in a small boat while wearing formal clothes was quite effective. Henri sat sleepily in his chair while the soldiers made their reports, and not until Joan herself returned to center stage did he resume interrupting and carrying on again.

The time was now apparently dusk, because the mime who represented the fire sprang up from the circle of rocks, his flame-fingers moving up, carrying their combustion and light up out of the coals and making the faces of the seated soldiers conscious of their weariness. Soon the army was asleep, and Joan herself lay down with them.

But here the action stopped. Henri began a convulsion of spleen and annoyance. Something was terribly wrong, but I couldn't guess what it was. Henri pointed at his watch and howled. One of the players on the stage started some kind of explanation, but Henri cut him off with a stream of what sounded like filthy words. As time went by and everyone waited, I gradually made out that one of the players who was needed for this scene was absent.

In one of his urgent looks toward the door, Henri's eyes fell on me. He looked away, then looked back. He smiled. Then he spoke to me, across all those empty chairs, but of course I didn't understand a word.

Henley dropped down off the stage and came back to where I was sitting. "He wants you to take one of the parts," she told me. "Stupid Emilio probably forgot all about it. We need somebody to be the Dauphin for five minutes. Will you do it?"

I followed her back to the stage. We climbed the steps and walked between all the sleeping soldiers.

"Here is the idea, Daddy," she said. "Joan and her army here are planning to attack the Dauphin tomorrow in his fortified city, but really at this point we find out it's kind of a love-hate thing because while Joan is sleeping on the ground among her men, the Dauphin sneaks in alone and wakes her with a kiss. When she sees who it is, Joan draws this terrible little knife she keeps under her armor and puts it to the King's throat. She holds him at bay this way for a few moments, all the while trying to raise her army from sleep with her cries, but they're too tired to wake up. Then the Dauphin makes a move to try to reach into his tunic, and since she fears he has a weapon hidden there, they struggle. She's strong, but he's stronger, so finally he gets this thing out, which is really the key to his garrison tied on a thong around his neck. Slowly she gets the idea, that he's come here to betray his own forces, and she lets him put the key around her own neck. He falls on his knees, he kisses her wrists. Then he sneaks off, and the scene is over with her standing among the sleeping army."

Just as Henley had promised, I was back in my folding chair again five minutes later, watching the action move into the events of the following day in the royal city. My scene seemed to have gone well enough, but of course I knew I couldn't tell. Henri thanked me in poor English before we left.

Nine

I understand why Henley and her friends called the loft where they lived the "Annex." It was nearly as bare and vast as the school itself, and lacked only a stage in duplicating the school's facilities. The same grey gym mats were spotted around on the floor. Old pieces of furniture pushed against the walls were heaped with clothing. The crayon murals on the walls were evidently part of the scenery of past productions. In front of the oil stove in the kitchen was a long table surrounded by ten or so chairs, and above the table hung a trapeze, supported by high ceiling beams. There was a long entrance hall giving onto four or more bedrooms before you reached the kitchen and eating room. Several people were already

there when Henley and I came in. I heard singing and lute
playing behind a closed door.

In the eating room, Henley removed a skirt and a pair
of panties from the seat of an armchair. "Silvia!" she
shouted in a musical tone. The lute playing stopped and a
barefoot girl came and claimed her clothes. When Silvia
disappeared again, Henley indicated that I should sit
down in the armchair.

"Let me get you something to drink, Daddy," she said.
"I'm sorry we don't have any alcoholic things. How about
a citron?"

"Fine," I said.

She went into the kitchen. I could see her through the
doorway taking down the citron bottle from an open shelf.

"Do you mind having it in a cup?" she asked me. "The
glasses are all dirty."

She poured a little of the citron into two cups and cut
it with water from the tap.

There was an open window just in front of me. "I like
your view," I said.

Henley returned with the citrons, handed me one, and
sat on a frayed leather hassock. "Yes," she said, "It's nice. You
can only see rooftops, but in Paris the rooftops look good."

"How many of you are there?"

"Eight, I think," she said. "There are always more in
the winter and less in the summer. People go places in the
summer."

"Are you all Americans?"

"Oh, no," she said. "Silvia's an American, and Peaches
is an American, and Wolf's an American, and I'm an
American, but then we have a French girl and boy, a
Swiss girl, an Italian man, and a German man."

"That's nine," I said.

"The French boy isn't here any more. Eight."

The door opened and two young men came down the hall. I remembered seeing them at the school earlier in the afternoon. One was thin and quiet, but the other, wearing flared leather trousers, whistled raucously. As they came into the eating room, the thin one collapsed on the threadbare couch amid the piles of clothes. The whistler came up behind Henley.

"Ah, Henley," he said, "Just the person I wanted to see. Tell me," he bent over, extended his hand, and cupped her right breast, "how's righty?"

"*Stop* it," Henley told him. "You're molesting me in front of my *father!*"

"Oh, a thousand pardons," this fellow said. "How absolutely crude. Hey, that's not your father, that's our King."

"He's also my father," Henley said. "Daddy, this is Wolf. He lives here. I don't like him very much."

"Well, fuck you very much," said Wolf, rapping his heels together and making a deep bow to her. He sat down on the floor beside my chair, hugging his knees with his arms. "Hey, man," he said to me, "do you know how good you were? You were very, very good."

The thin man on the couch lifted his face up to speak. "Don't bullshit him," he said in a thick accent. "He *was* good. Many times better than Emilio, the shithead."

"I'm trying to say that, I'm trying to tell him he was good. What did I say wrong? You didn't hear me. You had your head covered up with Peaches' pants."

"Are these from Peaches?" the thin man said, holding up some of the garments. He sniffed them. "Yes."

"I want this lewd behavior stopped," Henley said. "Otherwise I'm taking my father into my room."

"Don't do that," Wolf said. "We want to talk to him. What's that you've got?"

"In this cup?" Henley said. "Bug juice."

"Any left for us?"

"No," Henley told him.

Wolf got up and went into the kitchen. He emptied the rest of the citron bottle into a cup, sloshed some water into it, and returned.

"Hey, could we get him an Equity card or whatever?" he asked his friend. "I want him in the gig instead of that asshole Emilio. I know Henri would go for it, too. Now that I've seen it done right, I don't ever want to see Emilio up there again."

"My father's only here for a couple of days," Henley said.

"Aw, is that right?" Wolf asked. "Shit. How long?"

"I have to leave the day after tomorrow," I told him.

"Couldn't you stay another week? We open with this thing for six performances next Thursday. Why don't you wire your office that something big has come up. As far as we're concerned it has. You."

"I'm flattered that you think it went as it was supposed to this afternoon," I said, "but I'm afraid there isn't any way I can delay leaving."

"It didn't go as it was supposed to," Wolf said. "It went as *you wanted* it to. It was all yours, man."

Later in the evening, we ate together at the long dinner table. By this time, the others had all come back: Lise, a pretty blonde from Zurich; Marie, a dark Parisian; and Emilio, who spoke little English but endured a great deal of half-serious kidding. A place was set at the table for Peaches, but she never showed up. Since Henley was one of the cooks, she was late coming to the table, and there-fore I had to introduce myself to several of the people who came in to eat. They were very pleasant to me. The meal was a kind of pasta dish I didn't recognize, but it tasted fine and I had a fair-sized portion. There was also a green salad that I helped myself to twice. Lise and Silvia left the table as soon as they were finished eating. It was Emilio's turn to wash the dishes, and the others promised to kick his ass if he broke any. A kind of chocolate pudding was spooned out and eaten before Emilio reluctantly began his chores.

Peaches came in when only Wolf, Henley, and I were left at the table. She was still wearing her handkerchief top and her faded jeans, but there were grass stains on the knees of her jeans which hadn't been there earlier.

"Look at this," she said to us, pointing at the grass stains. "I fell. These pants are going to be ruined now. You can never clean grass stains out."

"Take them off and I'll work on them for you," Henley said. "I know how to get grass stains out."

Peaches sorted through the clothing on the couch. When she found a pair of purple velvet trousers that suited her, she removed her jeans and put on the purple trousers. There were magenta panties under the jeans. Before she could get the belt fastened, Wolf, who was just leaving the room, reached over and snapped the elastic of her panties. She pushed his hand away.

"Gee, you're beautiful," he said.

"I know."

"I'd stay if I had the time. But I'm late."

"Sure," said Peaches. "I understand. You big mother-grabbing bully."

"You said it," Wolf came back. "Grabbing you *is* like grabbing somebody's mother."

Wolf picked up an apple from the bowl in the center of the table. He walked down the long hall, and then we heard the door close behind him. Peaches pulled up one of the chairs and sat down at the table. I noticed for the first time, perhaps in the new light of Wolf's wisecrack, that she was older than any of the other students living here. I approximated her age as somewhere midway between my daughter's and my own.

"Hello again," she said to me. "So we meet in real life."

"I guess we do," I answered.

"You were very good this afternoon. It's such a relief to work with somebody who knows what he's doing."

Peaches brushed her hair back and tucked it behind an ear. It was a reddish-brown color, and shorter than the fashionable length; I hadn't seen it earlier because it had been under Joan's helmet.

"Henley, dear," she proposed, "What are the chances you could persuade your friend to join the company, just until next Saturday? I know I could get Henri to put him in the show permanently. He could make that scene believable. As it is now, with Emilio, it's a dreadful joke."

"Shhh," Henley whispered. "Emilio's right in the kitchen. And besides, this isn't my friend, it's my father."

"Oh, how do you do?" Peaches said to me. "I suppose we haven't met formally as yet. I'm Bernice Piluski." She extended her hand over the table.

"Ira Foxglove," I said, leaning over to shake her hand.

"Well, whether you're Henley's father or not, you're a talented mime, and the offer still stands. Will you help us?"

"You know, it's funny," Henley remarked. "Wolf just said almost the same thing you did to him, practically word for word."

"Wolf wanted to put him in the show?"

"Yes."

"Well, Wolf isn't as simple as I thought he was. Did he agree to do it?"

"He has to leave in a couple of days," Henley said.

"I'm sorry to hear that," Peaches said.

"But maybe I can do something for you before I leave," I told her. "I mean, if you're going to rehearse any more."

"Maybe you can," Peaches said.

At her request, we kept Peaches company while she spooned herself out some of what remained of the pasta and salad. Emilio made a fuss in Italian until Peaches assured him that she would be responsible for cleaning up her own dishes. Outside, the color of the sky was changing slowly but continuously. The air above the chimneys and roofs, which the humidity of the city had prevented from being blue earlier in the afternoon, was now becoming a soft salmon, apparently without effort, as if this shade were close to its natural color. The front door of the apartment closed behind someone often enough to make us the last ones left inside—even Emilio put on his fine things and went out into the city evening.

"Let's take your father for a walk," Peaches said from the kitchen as she was rinsing her plate.

"Are you talking to me?" Henley asked.

"Yes."

"Well, I don't know," Henley said. "Maybe he's tired."

Peaches dried her hands on a towel and came out of the kitchen. "Are you tired? You don't look tired to me."

Faced with this flattering report, I agreed that we should go out and look at Paris. Peaches excused herself and came back five minutes later wearing a white nylon sweater with a turtleneck. Her arms were thin and languid

in the long sleeves. Certain kinetic effects verified that
she wore no bra. We locked the apartment door behind us
and clattered down the stairs, crossing the landings which
swept us around the turns of our gliding, arcing path to
the street. Henley was first, followed by Peaches and me,
with the rhythm in Peaches' motions as she stepped down
from stair to stair, one hand on the railing, precisely
echoed in flops of her breasts.

Outside, we found the evening and its subtle lights an
exotic prospect. We walked on sidewalks made of paving
stones to a Metro station, and there descended into the
warmer air and harsher sounds of the subway. I pressed
one of my colorful bills on Henley, and she bought us all
first-class tickets. We arrived at our platform gate just as a
train was coming into the station. I was alarmed when I
saw the big mechanically driven gates close to bar us from
the platform. Henley explained that they would open
again when the train left. This seemed intuitively wrong
to me, but since it was something Henley obviously had
no control over, I didn't cross-examine her about it. As
she promised, when the train closed its doors and rolled
away, the platform gates opened.

We caught the next train, which came several minutes later. Inside the car, Henley pointed out the seats re-
served for war cripples. Although it was difficult to make
myself heard over the grinding mechanical noises, I asked
her whether any old cripple at all could use those seats, or
if it were necessary to prove you were a war cripple. I had
my question answered for me when a lady with a shopping
basket sat down in one of the seats, just under an advertisement for a film called *Amérique Fantastique*. In this
film, incidentally, if the pictorial prospectus was to be
believed, you could hope to learn the inside story on

Americans and all their restless sexuality. Two men and a girl, for example, were hard at it on the grass under the mysterious, silver St. Louis peace arch. Other insets in the advertisement showed California motorcyclists perched upon lavishly deformed Harley-Davidsons. All of which goes to prove, I decided, that imaginary landscapes are wherever you aren't.

We left the train at Montmartre, and there I was glad to find an escalator to carry us to the street. A mild pain had returned to my chest, forcing me to resolve to avoid stair-climbing for the rest of the evening if possible. On the street, people passing by in Harvard Square outfits moved in both directions on the narrow sidewalks; the evening was cool enough so that we saw capes fluttering like bats. The red light had almost left the western sky. Logical, geometric blue shadows extended until they would ultimately overlap each other everywhere. We paused and sat on the steps of some cathedral or other while the sun finished setting, then walked on in the night.

In Place Pigalle, we stopped and looked at the pictures advertising several "exotic revues." Under these theater marquees, whose thousands of wasted watts flashed names, times, and prices over our heads, we examined photographs of what we could expect to see inside. I suggested we go in.

"They'll take all your money, Daddy," Henley said.

"The sign says it's only about three dollars a head."

"That's for a ticket to get in. But these places are bars, and you have to drink. That's where they get you."

"Oh, let's do it," Peaches said. "I've been here two years, and I've never been in one of these dives."

"They aren't much, I'll tell you," Henley said. "They're only here for American and Japanese businessmen."

Over Henley's protestations, I bought three tickets and presented them to an Algerian ticket-taker in a blue silk costume. He led us down a short hall. Here we encountered a red velvet curtain, which the Algerian drew aside for us.

The room where the spectacle was to take place was totally black. The Algerian produced a flashlight, by which he guided our feet to a table, where we awkwardly sat down. Then, like the conjurer his costume told us he was, he caused a price list written on a piece of cardboard to materialize out of the blackness all around us. The flashlight beam from his one hand caught the card in his other, so that a spot of light floated in front of us with words written on it:

Whisky	nf 7.50
Cognac	nf 5.00
Bière	nf 5.00

We ordered three beers. This made the Algerian go away, but since he took the flashlight with him, we were left in total darkness. Henley held my hand tightly.

"Well, they're not giving the booze away," I said.

"I told you so," Henley said.

Peaches lit a cigarette. In the light of the match, we could see more of the table we were seated at (it was round, wet with the rings of earlier glasses, and carved by penknives) but we could see very little else. When the match went out, there was only the ember at the very end of Peaches' cigarette to see by.

"So far, I'm not disappointed," I said. "It reminds me of the beginning of any number of traveling salesman jokes."

The Algerian came back with his flashlight, installing a new set of people with each trip. On one of his journeys he brought us our beer, for which I paid him royally.

"I didn't know you knew any traveling salesman jokes," Henley said.

"I do."

"Tell a couple while we're waiting."

"No," I said. "They're not very funny."

A spotlight came on, revealing that a corner of the room, which was bare of tables and chairs, had been arranged with a cardboard set to look something like the interior of an airplane cockpit. The light reflected from this set gave us our first view of the rest of the room, which was crammed with tables, most of them empty. Even after this spot came on, we still had a longish wait while the Algerian ensured that everyone had been served and thereby relieved of at least five new francs.

The needle hit the surface of a scratchy record, and suddenly we were numbed with a medley of French aviation songs played at a clearly unsafe volume level. After the medley had played through once, it was started again, and with it, the show.

The premise for this first skit, not completely un-believable, was that pilots and stewardesses are often up to no good in the front of the airplane, away from the prying eyes of the passengers. The actor who played the pilot in this case began the flight attending to his duties but soon became tortuously distracted by the stewardess/stripper, whose subtle and sly breasts were soon in full view. Each time the pilot would leave his seat in pursuit of the temptation, a rising, screaming sound would tell you that the plane was going into a dive, and the pilot had to reach back to the controls, only to be teased and frustrated again. I'll have to admit here that although the comedy was clumsy and I never discovered what the audience found to laugh at, my feelings were not completely untouched by what I was seeing. The skillful stewardess did things with her hands in rubbing, flowing motions over her own pelvis which caught my attention no less than that of her captain, and although I was prepared to be blasé about a male character in a strip show, for a few moments his agony was mine. The skit ended in a clap of cymbals as the pilot lunged for his nude temptress, missed her completely, and was swept out the open door into the free space behind the set.

We sat through three more of these little playlets. I'm ashamed to say I found each more stimulating than the last, although even more absurd. Before the evening was over, we had to endure a story about a voluptuous Little Red Riding Hood in simulated copulation with a simulated wolf. Throughout the last sequence, I was less puzzled by any mystery in the story than by a more realistic, or at least practical, question: Was Peaches intentionally allowing her leg to rest against mine in the darkness under the table? The coincidence of this real touch through the dark when everything around us was a sexual mirage went straight to some inner quick of mine I hadn't been aware of for a long time. I surprised myself by wanting to bite somebody's nipples, it didn't matter whose.

The Metro which took us back to the Annex was filled with lovers. As we walked from the Metro station over the paving stones through the soft night, I had one of my ladies on each arm. At the Annex, we rested at each landing on the stairs spiraling up to the top floor, since the effort of climbing was making me breathless.

Through windows thoughtfully provided, we could see at each stage how our progress brought us higher and let us see farther out into Paris.

When we reached the top of the stairs, Peaches invited us into her room for a tomato juice nightcap.

"O.K.," I said, "You talked us into it."

But it turned out that Henley wasn't interested. She went off to make up a cot for me in the eating room.

"Then you come by yourself," Peaches suggested, and I did.

Her room was scrupulously clean and well ordered, compared with the rest of what I had seen of the Annex. I sat in a chair at the foot of her bed while she went out to the kitchen to get the tomato juice. When she returned, she arranged herself on her bed while we drank the tomato juice from pleasant old French glasses.

"Have you been living here about the same length of time as Henley?" I asked.

"Longer. I was here when she came from that college in the South she dropped out of. Template, or whatever."

"That wasn't the name."

"That's what she told us."

"She was kidding," I said.

Peaches sipped her tomato juice. "She wasn't having a very good time when she first came here. I think she's enjoying it more now. She's very well liked."

"What was the matter when she first came?" I asked.

"Oh, I think she got a letter that upset her. From a boy in America she was involved with."

"Ah," I said.

"Apparently they had been pretty serious about each other, but this guy wrote and said he was reluctantly informing her that he had caught the clap from her and that

she should go and get herself checked before her brains
rotted out. It turned out she didn't have it. But the letter
made her pretty upset."

"I can well imagine," I said.

"You didn't know about it?"

"No."

"Well, I hope I haven't betrayed a confidence by
telling you. There wasn't much to it. She found out she
was clean, as I said."

"That's good."

We sipped our tomato juice in silence for a while.

"I really shouldn't have brought that subject up,"
Peaches said.

"It's all right," I told her.

"What about you?" she asked me. "Do you really have
to go back to London so soon?"

"Oh, yes."

"To your wife?"

"Yes," I said. I sat back in my chair. "I guess you know
about me, then."

"Henley told us about your heart attack and about
your wife leaving you. But she didn't say anything about
you as a person. About your talent, or anything."

"She's the one who has the talent," I said.

"Well, of course she has talent," Peaches said, "or she
couldn't get into this school. I have talent, for that matter.
Probably less than Henley, although we're trying to do different things. But you're better than she is. You have a gift."

"I really don't see how you can say that on the basis of
something that took me less than five minutes to do."

"Five minutes is long enough for some things,"
Peaches said. "I'll tell you a story about something that
happened to me in five minutes sometime." She drained

the last bit of tomato juice from the bottom of her glass, then handed it to me. "Here," she said. "Let's not make Henley nervous. We can talk some more tomorrow."

I took the glasses to the sink in the kitchen where I ran water into them. In the eating room, the sheets Henley had put on my cot were a luminous white where they reflected the moonlight from the open window. As I took off my clothes, another in the long series of fitful erections that had tormented me this evening nearly prevented me from removing my pants. I put my hand around my ridiculously swollen cock and squeezed it.

Once, just after Henley was born, Portia and I took our new baby to Franklin Park Zoo, and there we walked through light snow on a grey winter day to the monkey house. As Henley's carriage wheels dripped dirty water on the tiles, we looked in through the bars, and there a male was raging against the walls and dropping down on the backs of his fellow creatures, hissing with ardor, his penis a stiff red worm. Portia gripped my arm. "My God, Ira," she said. "I hope you never get like that."

T e n

The next morning, Henley made breakfast for me while the rest of the Annex slept. She found a box of oatmeal no one had looked at for two years, but amazingly enough, it tasted fine. As I've already mentioned, I like oatmeal well enough to eat it any time of day, but in the morning, it can be exquisite when properly prepared. Henley and I have been around each other long enough that she can make oatmeal very satisfactorily. You have to keep stirring it so that the consistency isn't gluey or lumpy but just right.

"What were you and Peaches talking about for so long?"

"Not much," I said. "The mime school, life in Paris."

"Did she tell you about herself?"

"No."

"That's funny. She usually gets around to herself right off the bat."

"I think she promised she would. She said she'd tell me later about some short incident that made a lot of difference to her."

"A short incident?" Henley said. "What would that be?" She went to the refrigerator and brought me a glass of milk for my oatmeal. "I think I know," she said. "Do you want me to tell you?"

"Why don't you," I said. "Then when Peaches decides she's going to tell me, I can stop her and say I've heard it already."

"Very well," Henley said. She sat down in the chair next to mine and leaned forward.

"Before you start," I said. "Could we arrange things so your hair doesn't fall in my porridge?"

"Oh, excuse me," Henley said. She wiped off the hair that had gotten dipped in my bowl. "Here, let me trade you. There's more in the pot."

But I made her leave my bowl alone. "This is still perfectly good," I said. "I'm planning to eat what's left in the pot anyway. Start the story."

Henley washed the sticky part of her hair under the tap, then came back and sat beside me again. "I don't guarantee this is true, I'll just tell you what Peaches told us."

"Fine," I said.

"This was supposed to have happened when she was fifteen years old, on her grandfather's farm in Missouri. She claims her grandfather had this big farm, and she was allowed to ride the horses since she was very young. She rode the horses fast, through the fields and under the trees. It was practically her job, taking these horses out and giving them a thrill by letting them run their heads off with her clinging to their backsides. Have you got the picture?"

"Yep," I said.

"And the other thing you have to know is that she was a virgin. She always puts that fact in when she tells the story, so I wouldn't dare leave it out."

"Got it," I said.

"Well, there she was one morning, whizzing through the tall grass, on her way to the river where the forest trail began, riding her favorite horse. Let's call him Trigger. Isn't that a suitable name? Trigger. Wow. I bet that's what his name really was. Can't you just see it? Horses don't get named Trigger for nothing." Henley put her hand up to her mouth and blew a snicker into it. "Oh, I can't tell you this," she said. "You'll have to ask Peaches yourself."

"Come on," I said. "Now that you've started it, you have to finish."

"O.K.," Henley said, returning to a sober mood. "We have Peaches and Trigger as I said. But also another character, who I'll call Melvin the Moron. I think Peaches said this was a cousin of hers. Anyway, another part of the premise is that he was secretly keen on Peaches. And that he had a slingshot."

"You'd better get to the point," I said. "I think I hear someone getting up."

"The point is that Melvin stationed himself in a tree along Peaches' route, and when she came by underneath, ZOT! He knocked her off her horse with his slingshot."

"Is that the end of the story?"

"No. There she was, dehorsed, and knocked out, if I remember, and so he had his way with her. It doesn't sound like much when I tell it, but she makes it much more of a big deal. You're supposed to visualize Peaches as a ripe maiden, bounding along through that green countryside, the horse's hooves going clippity-clop and the saddle going creakity-creak, and then WHACK, old Melvin picks her off with his slingshot and does the job on her. A short courtship."

"What happened to her then?"

"Then she grew up, went to a midwestern college, was the first person in the history of her school to get in trouble with drugs, married a guy who started his own electronics company, and ditched him two years ago to come here and become a great artiste. Now let's change the subject, because here she comes."

"Hey," I said. "That story wasn't completely funny."

But then Peaches came into the room, and sat with me over a cup of coffee while I finished my oatmeal. The other denizens of the Annex drifted in and out of the kitchen, taking away with them pieces of fruit or slices of bread spread with honey which served as breakfast. This morning, Peaches was wearing an Indian print blouse, shorts, and sandals. Perhaps because she was smiling so much, perhaps because she was the only one in the house besides Henley who was paying any attention to me, I thought she looked quite beautiful. And so I was pleased when it worked out that Henley had to be at the school this morning, but Peaches was free and would be able to go along with me and help with some small shopping matters in the city.

We walked out over the cobblestones under blue, dry air which had come in during the night from Scandinavia. Taxis and buses worked their way through the streets, taking their places in today's traffic jam. As we went by a construction project, some of the workmen stared at Peaches' walk, which was articulated enough to be full of visual rewards. The Metro took us to the Boulevard Haussman, where we found the sidewalk almost completely choked with people. I'll swear that the temperature felt a full ten degrees hotter here than in the part of the city we had just left. The level of noise from people and machines was similarly intensified. I was looking for a watchband for Portia's watch, among other things, and Peaches took me to a large department store where she thought we might have some luck.

The floors of the department store were only slightly less crowded than the street. Many of the people buying things were recognizable archetypes: Texas ladies in pink pantsuits wearing diamond bracelets and so forth.

"I don't know why anybody would come all the way here from the U.S. just to spend their time in a department store," I said.

"I can't think why either," Peaches said. "But the only place you'll find more tourists this morning is the Champs Elysées. There everyone is at work with a camera. At least here you don't get people scowling at you for walking through their picture."

We rode an elevator to the third floor. Peaches led the way to the jewelry section, where I found a perfectly good watchband for Portia for about the same money we had paid for our beer the previous evening. After Peaches had helped me pay and receive my change, we walked on a little farther, through the children's wear section and on into the ladies' wear.

"This place is about as plain as an American department store," I said. "Look at all this vinyl and chrome."

"Well, what did you expect?"

"I'm not sure," I said. "I don't think I expected quite so much plastic."

"Department stores are the same everywhere," Peaches said. "Is there anything else you want here, or shall we go?"

"I want to just check this women's section," I told her. We walked up and down the aisles and looked around, but I didn't find what I was looking for.

"What is it?"

"Oh, I'm looking for this stuff called Feather Fabric. It's a new material clothes are being made out of. The fibers are really little balloons. You have to blow them up with a gas bottle. When the fabric is deflated, you can store a whole blouse or a dress in a small capsule. It comes packaged in a container about the size of a lipstick, and that includes the gas bottle too."

"I've seen that somewhere," Peaches said. "It's very new, isn't it?"

"It's been for sale in America for a year or so, but I believe it's just been introduced over here."

"We aren't going to find something like that here," Peaches said. "We'll have to go to a fancier store."

The elevator took us down to the street level, where we left the timid air conditioning and walked out onto the crowded sidewalk again. We walked several blocks before Peaches led the way into an expensive women's clothing store.

"I see it," I said.

There was a small display of Feather Fabric blouses on one of the counters. We walked over and looked at them.

"Wow," said Peaches, "I've never seen anything that looked like that." She leaned over and touched the sleeve of one of the blouses. "It changes color!" she said.

"Not really," I told her. "It doesn't have any color of its own. It's iridescent, like a peacock's feather. It makes a color depending on how thick it is, by interference effects."

"It looks kind of blue, but there are shiny blacks and reds depending on where you stand," Peaches said. "But this one over here is almost transparent."

"That one is exactly the same as this one," I said. "The only difference between them is the inflation pressure. Here, I'll show you."

I attached the gas capsule to the inflation manifold of one of the blouses. "See, it has this little knob you turn to set the inflation pressure. At a high pressure, the fibers are all big and you get the iridescent effect. Also, you see, the colors gradually disappear and the fabric becomes very sheer."

Peaches felt the blouse between her fingers. "It's nearly invisible now."

"Then you can let all the gas out, roll it up, and store it in its little container." I showed her how to take the top off and put the blouse away in its capsule.

"Amazing," Peaches said. "But what are you supposed to do about cleaning it?"

"Nothing," I said.

"What do you mean?"

"It cleans itself."

"How does it do that? Inside the capsule, or something?"

"No," I said. "Outside the capsule. Feel this inflated one. Doesn't it feel kind of slippery? The inflation gas slowly diffuses through the walls of the balloon fiber, so that when any oil or dirt gets on the fiber, it gets shed, like a snake skin. If you get a hard spot of something on it, you're supposed to break it up by pinching it, and then the little pieces fly off by themselves."

"It really never gets dirty?"

"Nope."

While Peaches marveled over the Feather Fabric, I looked around for the price. I was dismayed when I found it. Peaches had been right in guessing that Feather Fabric would be an expensive commodity. I brought out my wallet, counted out enough money to buy two blouses, and handed it to the salesgirl, after indicating what I wanted.

"This is the most fantastic material I've ever held in my hands," Peaches said. "The next time I have any money, I'm going to come back here and buy some more. Does it last very long? I'd think it would get holes in it and be spoiled."

"It's pretty strong," I said, "But they give you a patching kit with it, in case it gets a big leak. It's just some goo that seals off the leaking fibers. You can hardly see the repair if it's done properly."

"Say, how come you know so much about this stuff?"

The salesgirl came back with my change, which I put in my pocket. The two blouse capsules in their fancy boxes were put into a white paper bag and handed to me.

"Because," I told Peaches as we left the counter, "I invented it."

We had our lunch at a large outdoor restaurant near l'Opéra. Peaches put the bag of fresh tomatoes she had just bought from a pushcart man in the middle of our table. We each ate a tomato while we waited for our food to be served.

"I haven't decided to believe you yet. About inventing that Feather Fabric. You'd be rich by now, wouldn't you? Maybe you are rich."

"'Fraid not," I said. My mouth was full of tomato.

Our table was close to the street. Trucks went by only a few feet from Peaches' back as she sat facing me. "Why not?" she asked.

"Because I sold the invention to a guy who figured out how to make money with it. It's his now. He doesn't owe me a cent on it."

"Did he pay you a good price for it?"

"It seemed like a good price at the time."

"How much?"

"Five hundred dollars."

Peaches was silent. She looked up at the other eaters, then down at the bag of tomatoes.

"I'd say you got screwed," she said.

"Oh, well," I told her. "Win a few, lose a few. That's baseball."

A sour expression here from Peaches.

"In any case, it wasn't the guy who bought the invention who wronged me. Anything that happened to me I did to myself. I had to plead with him to get him to buy it. At the time, I was convinced the project was a failure."

"How do you mean?"

"I had an entirely different purpose in mind. I was trying to develop a material that could be used for the bedclothes and possibly even for the bandages of serious burn victims. You can't use ordinary materials like cotton in these cases because the wound sticks to the fabric. I was hoping to make a self-cleaning fabric that wouldn't do that."

"Didn't you tell me earlier that Feather Fabric is self-cleaning?"

"It is, provided you can fragment the dirt, by pinching it or rubbing it, as I said. But that's just what you can't do to the solid structure of a wound while it's healing. I found that although each of the individual balloon fibers stays

clean, the clotted blood would organize around the inter-
locking shapes of the fibers, so that the clot would stick
anyway. It took me three years to develop a fabric that
wasn't any more use to a burned child than an ordinary
cotton sheet."

The waiter served our omelettes and white wine.
Peaches moved her bag of tomatoes to another chair to
make room.

"I was just trying to remember," she said. "Henley suffered burns as a child, didn't she? I think she still has some
scars on one leg."

"Yes, that's right," I said. "Henley was playing with
some children, and somebody had his father's cigarette
lighter. They were trying to put fuel in it, and accidentally
lit it after the fuel had spilled on Henley's leg."

"So you were trying to make this special cloth to help
her."

"Oh, no," I said. "At the time, I acted as helpless as
everyone else. We just had to let her get better by herself.
As it was, her burns weren't so extensive that she couldn't
lie down. Some of the other children who were with her in
the hospital were much worse off. It was in visiting them
that I became aware of the need for such a cloth."

"And so, seeing the need, you just went home and
started working on it?"

"More or less."

"Why? I mean, what made you think you could do it?"

"I had the idea. One day, riding home on the bus from
the hospital, I thought about a fabric made from balloons
woven into threads. I searched around and found that
nothing like the fibers I would need were available com-
mercially, so I began trying to make my own. As far as I
can tell, ideas always show up like that, absolutely free.

And very often in a nearly final form. That is, they're all clothed and have hair and adult teeth—you hardly ever have to do anything to them or wait for them to grow up. What you do have to do is test them, with your education or with your experience, to see whether they're any good. You can go to school or grow old learning how to test ideas. That takes hard work. But no one can teach you how to get them. They come for nothing."

"And since they come for nothing," Peaches said, cutting into her omelette, "you don't mind giving them away."

I finished eating the forkful I had started and sipped my wine before answering. "No," I said. "It's just the opposite. I hate like hell having an idea turn out to be wrong or impractical. That's about the only way you can lose an idea, by discarding it."

"Or you can sell it."

"All right," I said. "Selling an idea is a little more complicated. To start with, you can't ever sell just a raw idea. You always have to do a certain amount of work on an invention before anybody will buy it. You have to show that it works. And so if you do sell something, it's more like you're selling the work than the idea. Is this making any sense?"

"Sure," Peaches said. "I think."

"But I suppose I haven't really answered your question. You wanted to know why I started working on the project in the first place. Was that what you asked me?"

"I don't remember if I asked that, but that's what I wanted to know."

I put down my fork and sat back in my chair. "That's a hard question. You know, I think that if something had already existed that would do the job I wanted balloon fabric to do, I would have just cheerfully bought some to use in Henley's case. I might have said, 'Hm, tricky stuff,' or some such thing, but I never would have been very curious about it. Still, it would only be a matter of time before something else bothered me that I thought I could fix. Then I'd be wondering about that."

Peaches had finished her wine, so I refilled her glass. A silent breeze luffed her shirt.

"Do you try to fix everything that bothers you?"

"Everything mechanical. Or really, I should say I usually have some thought about mechanical things, even though I may not get to my feet and actually do it."

"I'm surprised," Peaches said. "From what I know of you up until now, I never would have guessed that your head was full of mechanical ideas."

"What did you think it was full of?"

"I didn't know," Peaches said. "If you were like me, you'd spend most of the time regretting things too far in the past to be changed. And then you'd spend some time with religious anxieties—I've lived most of my life very sure about things my mother wanted me to be sure of, only to doubt them now that I need them. Then the rest of the time you'd think about sex."

"Oh, I do think about sex."

Peaches had finished her meal and was using her napkin at the corners of her mouth.

"Everybody does," she said, more to the tablecloth than to me.

The waiter came then and I paid for our meal. It was pleasant to stand up. Other people were waiting for our table. They seemed displeased that the table was so close to the street and they complained to the waiter about it, but he ignored them.

I carried Peaches' bag of tomatoes as we started off for the school. When we came out from under the café awning, the high sun felt warm on my neck.

"What are you working on now?" Peaches asked me. "Do you have another project started?"

"Yes," I told her, "although started is the word. It isn't going as fast as I want it to."

"What is it?"

"It's a prosthetic heart. With its own power supply, a little closed-cycle steam engine, except it doesn't use steam."

"Wow," she said. "That takes my breath away."

"Why?"

"I mean, you're building your own heart. It's too freaking much."

We walked on for a while. "I wish it *wasn't* too freaking much," I said. "I'm not having much luck with it. The power supply seems to be working fine, but I haven't found any reasonable design for the pump itself. Or any good material, either. In some sense, the material question is the balloon fabric problem all over again. I have to find some substance that won't support thrombus formation. Otherwise, the pump would be plugged up in a day."

"You're fantastic," Peaches said, looking over at me as we walked around a construction site in the street. "What would you do if you found a good material? Build the pump and try it out in yourself?"

We walked on, avoiding trucks, workmen, and the hole they were making. "I shouldn't have told you," I said.

"Yes, you should have," she said. "It's just that I never met anyone who felt that he had to do so much by himself."

We rode several stops on one Metro line, then changed to another to reach the school. I was feeling tired and was considering going back to the Annex by myself to get a little rest. I decided it would be best to find Henley. I'd get directions from her on how to get back, and also to borrow her key. Peaches was silent as we climbed the long flights of stairs up to the school. By the time we reached the top floor, my ass was definitely dragging.

We opened the door and came in on an incoherent scene. The stage was dark, but room lights illuminated the remainder of the floor. The students sprawled in chairs. Some talked, others watched people rehearsing on the mats.

"What's going on?" I asked Peaches.

"Individual practice," she said. "And then later we do improvisations. They're fun. You ought to do one."

"I'm not feeling very well," I told her. "I don't believe I'll stay long. Do you see Henley anywhere?"

"Yes," she said. "She's sitting on a chair over by Henri's office."

"Ah," I said. "I see her. If you'll excuse me."

"Wait a minute. Don't go away mad. I didn't mean to say anything facetious about your work. In fact, I wanted to tell you something quite the opposite, that I think it's extraordinary. You're extraordinary. But I spoiled it."

"I'm not doing it because I consciously want to save myself," I said.

"Why, then?"

"Oh, I don't know, I don't know. That never seems like a question worth asking. How, maybe, but not why. For all I know, you could be right. I could be doing it for myself. But that makes so little difference. Whether I only want to succeed or whether I really need to won't determine whether I do or not."

"What will?"

"That," I said, "would be lovely to know."

I left Peaches and walked to the corner of the room where Henley and her friends were working on their *St. Joan* parts. Henley was busy when I reached her. In this scene, she was one of the soldiers in the opposing army. When the battle begins, it became clear why they were practicing this sequence on the mats. In the shifting patterns of the battle, the mimes coordinated their action so that your eye was first taken here to one man's plight and then smoothly there to another's. It was as if the focus of attention, which was never in more than one place at the same time, were being played back and forth in a continuous volley. Henley fell heavily in her turn, and then made her exit.

"Hi, Daddy," she said. "Did you have your lunch? I wasn't sure whether you were coming back to the Annex for lunch or not."

"No, we ate in a restaurant," I said. "But as a matter of fact, I'm planning to go back to the Annex now and curl up for the rest of the afternoon."

"Aren't you feeling well?"

"Not particularly. I'm just tired."

Henley looked disappointed. "Can you wait a little while?" she asked me. "I can go back with you after I've done my improvisation."

"O.K.," I said. "When do you do that?"

"We're starting them now."

A light went on above the stage. The students came to the end of their conversations, picked up their chairs, and began moving toward the stage. Henley and I let ourselves bob along with them.

"What's this all about?" I asked her. "What do you improvise?"

"Each person gets fifteen minutes or so to tell something without words. It's usually autobiographical. Just as an example, Peaches has given us I don't know how many slightly different versions of how she got knocked off the horse and raped."

Henley and I sat on the floor near the stage.

"I should have a chance to go on near the beginning," she said in a low voice.

"Does everyone have to do it?"

"No," she said. "You only do it if you want to. It's sort of like confession."

The first improvisation was by a female member of the class I hadn't met. She was thin and young. Her pale yellow hair came together in a slender braid that lay restlessly on her back. This girl's story, in which she took the parts of several people, began with a narration of what one could hear through the open windows of her apartment building. By her action, we were encouraged to visualize a man and a woman engaged in a lusty brawl. One by one, this fighting couple were visited by the other occupants of the building, who begged, commanded, threatened them, but they wouldn't be quiet. The occupants of the building assembled to discuss the problem. At last, a course of action was agreed upon. They would send a gift to the warring couple, a pistol, which one of the partners could use to shoot the other, thus ending the argument. But when the pistol was delivered, the sight of it frightened the couple into an amorous reconciliation, with an ironic consequence: they now made love as loudly as they had fought before.

This was a hard act for Henley to follow. Her improv-isation, which was much shorter than the first one, in-troduced a stamp collector about to paste some new acquisitions into his stamp albums. Henley made us see the books, the stamps, and the paste: everything was laid out carefully and apparently the project was ready to go until the collector opened a window. On sitting down, the collector found that some of the stamps had been moved from their assigned places by a zephyr from the open window. Everything was laboriously replaced. The paste was taken out of its jar and applied to the backs of the stamps moments before a breeze lifted them up and stuck them in various places around the room. From here, the comedy descended lower and lower as the collector stuck first the fingers of one hand, then her foot, then her elbow, et cetera, to the sticky mass of stamps.

"That's enough, Henley," someone said offstage. "We get the idea."

As Henley stepped down, Henri spoke in rapid French to the rest of the group. Someone answered him from the floor, also in French: I believe this was Wolf. I heard my name mentioned. Henley dropped to the floor beside me.

"Are they talking about me?" I asked her.

"Yes."

"What are they saying?"

"Wolf wants you to do an improvisation. Peaches is agreeing with him."

Henri smiled at me from the stage. The students sitting in the folding chairs turned their shoulders to look at me.

"Do you want me to tell them you're sick?" Henley asked.

"No," I said. I stood up. "Don't tell them that. I'm not. Tell them I'm game."

I climbed the two steps to the stage and stood there, alone. How to begin? I didn't know. There was a single chair, so I sat. The students in the darkness looked at me and I looked back at them.

In winter, before our marriage, Portia and I walked alone in the country. The overcast, which had snow in it, hung above the white fields with their grass stubble, above sad, beautiful red barns. We left the road, climbing up over a ploughed mound of ice and road dirt. We followed a stream, finding it by the grey snow and dark spots, both close and in the distance, where the water was open. It led us under hemlocks where the branches were weighed so low that we had to bend down to pass under. Passing under took a long time.

And in fact, it was this sense of time, time passing as Portia and I, our gloves holding each other, passed under the trees. This was what I had wanted to get across to the class when I began to play my life in mime.

I could feel Portia's fingers through her white leather. Looking back at her. Her black hair and the white clouds. We walked straight between the hemlock stands where they would let us.

The class let us go on. Did they see where I was taking her? Or she was taking me? Into marriage, into childbirth, into heart disease. They didn't stop us. It didn't matter.

In snow, sitting beneath trees by water, I thought we were agreeing to love each other forever. Perhaps we were. With my glove removed, my hand was invited in from the cold. It accepted, a polite, sincere guest. And stayed the afternoon.

Forever? Henley was born. To show this to the class, I writhed on my back. It had been difficult for Portia. They were ready to cut her, it had taken so long. But finally, birth. The doctor smacked life into the new baby. It happened in the early morning, only just before dawn, at a time which would ordinarily be deepest sleep, where the nightmares come from. I rode with Portia in a taxi to the hospital, then walked the three miles home, through spectacularly empty downtown streets. I climbed Beacon Hill and sat for a few moments on the steps of the State House. Over my shoulder, the State House dome reflected the beginnings of the coming day.

But all this was invisible in the snow. There we were alone together for white hours. We lay as if on pale sheets, but it was impossible to take off our winter clothes. Instead...

Instead I researched Portia's body with my fingers, forcing my hand, like a plumber's snake, into blind spots. But of course, I couldn't tell this to the class, nor did it seem that they should know. I carried the story further on, into the heyday of Portia's swimming. I showed them Portia's half-risen athletic star. She worked so hard. She did well, too, in the competitions she thrust herself into, and certainly few other swimmers wanted to win more. But she was beaten by girls half her age. Henley grew, heavily in my company, and therefore developed points of view somewhat like mine.

But before she left me for good, I found I missed her more when she was in the next room than when she was far away. Once when I was still in good health, we walked together in a park by the ocean. I climbed a low tree—it was easy, it had branches near the ground—to experiment with these feelings, to see if loneliness would come as strongly when we were separated by only a few feet. From my branch, I reached down, and she reached up, but our fingers couldn't touch. The inches were as impossible as miles. From my tree, I could see ocean waves breaking on rocks.

The class had found it easy enough to see Portia and me as I conjured us forward in various stages of our young life. But I let them down, it seemed, when telling them about recent events. They didn't understand what feather fiber was ever intended to be, nor what it now was. And they were utterly baffled by my description of Neptune's blimp.

Eleven

I carried the bag of tomatoes for Peaches as we made our way back to the Annex alone. I wanted to lie down all through the dinner we had with Henley and her friends at a restaurant near the school. Peaches was tired too, she said, and declined the invitation to go with the others to the after-dinner party in favor of coming home.

Back at the Annex, we stopped at her bedroom door and I handed her the bag.

"Good night," I said.

"Why not come in?" Peaches asked, her hand fingering the door knob.

"Thanks, but I'm bushed. I plan to fix Portia's watch-band and hit the sack."

"You could do both in my room. I have a much more comfortable bed than yours. And I don't mind sharing it with you."

"That's kind of you, Peaches. But I really am feeling quite tired."

"Sure," she said.

I found Portia's watch in my pants pocket and the new watchband in an inside coat pocket. Having found these parts, plus the screwdriver on my penknife, I sat on the edge of my cot and began fitting the watchband to the watch. It didn't take long. That done, I switched off the light and fell asleep.

Something awakened me around 1 a.m. I got up and discovered that Henley and company were not yet home. I saw a light coming from under the door to Peaches' room. I got back in bed but couldn't sleep. I started thinking about Henley and her ideas about change: *things are always getting either better or worse.* But when things get worse, shouldn't you fight it? Shouldn't you take it personally? What would Portia say? She would talk about growth, because this she knows. Growth and inevitable death, but growth all the same.

And here I had a thought that came with the force of a collision. That a growing biological thing, perhaps a tomato, could provide the material I needed to finish my heart. Every type of artificial material, every plastic and steel, became clotted with blood sooner or later. But the skin of a tomato is living tissue.

Tomatoes are grown in the ground, where the rain reaches their roots. They can also be grown in a solution of water and food. Is it possible they could be grown in blood?

I might begin experiments testing the thrombogenicity of the outermost layers of the tomato skin. It could be that the plant skin was thrombus resistant by itself, or at least was a suitable basement membrane for the growth of animal endothelial tissue, which would certainly be nonthrombogenic.

I climbed out of bed in a fever with my new ideas. I needed a tomato and a few other things maybe Peaches could find for me. I found the tomato myself, still in the bag Peaches had left on the kitchen counter. Tomato in hand, I advanced forward to Peaches' door and rapped gently.

"Peaches?"

"Yes?"

Opening her door a crack, I saw Peaches stretched out on top of her bed, reading, and observed that she must like to sleep in the raw.

"Oh," I said, "I didn't mean to disturb you."

"You're not," she replied.

"I know it's late, but I couldn't sleep. I have an idea for an experiment I'd like to try now. With your help."

"It's not late. It's only one-fifteen. The kids probably won't be home for another two hours. It's okay, Ira. Come here," she said patting a spot next to her pillow, "and tell me how I can help you."

She arched herself up on one arm and lifted her face. Her nipples, large and erect, seemed to be jumping out at me.

"Umm, I'm not sure it's such a good idea," I croaked.

"Well then," she said, now kneeling on the bed, facing me. "You don't *have* to come *here*." Stepping off the bed she came toward me, not stopping until she was close enough to kiss me hard on the lips. I kissed her back.

Still holding the ripe tomato in one hand, I reached out and took one of her lovely breasts in my other hand. I supported it as I would a little puppy. As Peaches reached down to pick up the tomato that had, by now, fallen from my hand, she stuck her thumb clear through its center, and offered it to me between her breasts.

"Do you want to experiment on this?" she asked sweetly.

She titillated my useless male nipples with the tips and nails of her fingers. She made tiny orbits around the central, not-so-spectacular promontories.

"Could you give me a little more attention, please?" Peaches asked me.

"Sure," I said. "Although you seem to be doing fine by yourself."

"Don't be a miserable bastard."

"I can't help it. It's my nature."

She rolled away to the far side of the bed. Where she lay, for a moment, on her back, the spare and handsomely made shape of her abdomen broken, in its falling curve, only by her pubic forest. Which was red. And intercepting the light it received from the lamp, cast a low shadow over her thigh.

Peaches got up and lit a cigarette. When she sat down again, she said, "You're not interested? In getting laid by me?"

"Oh," I said, "I'm awfully interested in laying *somebody*. My wife, I think."

"But she's not here and I am," Peaches said. "Why don't you close your eyes and pretend I'm her?"

"That's what I was sort of doing."

"Well," said Peaches, grinding out her cigarette and pulling back the covers, "I don't care what you do. Just get your fat ass in gear and let's go."

"Should I turn the light out?"

"No, skip it." She was kneeling on the bed, facing me. Her breasts hung forward, distinguished from her other skin by their faint bluish lines and barely visible stretch marks. I reached out and took them in my hands.

"O.K.," she said. "That's a start, but I need some work down here, too." She guided my hand to her twat. "It could take some time, seeing as how you got me pissed off."

"Um," I said, "there's one thing. I don't think this should get too rough. My heart might stop."

"I'll keep that in mind," Peaches said. "But somehow I think you're going to be all right. Now work."

My middle and ring fingers went in to investigate while the rest of the hand waited outside. To my own agitations, Peaches slowly began to add hers. For a time, we marched on together in this way, sometimes in and sometimes out of step. Peaches lay back, keeping her heels under her buttocks. She made timely readjustments of my hand with her own. We jogged along, to my growing gratification and apparently to hers, for we hit an occasional bump that threatened to crack my knuckles.

With my left hand in conversation with her vagina, my right hand was free, but not for long. Peaches pressed it into service in the neighborhood of her anus. It was reluctant to volunteer for this assignment. Peaches' hand forced it to abandon modesty. Its middle finger found itself introduced to the subject: one, then two knuckles disappeared. Peaches lay still and breathed deeply. She held the wrist of my anal hand in a tight grip.

We started with a lurch. Leave the driving to us. We sped along. There was no time to get into Peaches before I reached my stop. I dropped my load all over the back of her leg.

"Oh, no," Peaches said. She looked around at me.

"Gee, I'm sorry," I said.

Peaches crawled off the bed. She wrapped herself in a robe and left the room. The tomato and I lay next to each other in disgrace. Man and fruit cast off. Brothers. Its seed and mine spilled, now mixed.

The open window behind me played a cool night breeze on my soggy cock. I felt acutely lonely for Portia.

Peaches returned from the bathroom. She came in, closed the door behind her, and surveyed the mess in the bed.

I got to my feet. The floor felt cold.

"I was just about to tidy things up," I told her.

"Don't bother," she said.

"It's no trouble, really," I said. I picked up the tomato. The texture of its skin had strangely changed. It was smooth and strong, somewhat like plastic, but much more supple and elastic. Most of the interior material had drained away, leaving the skin as a hollow, flexible bulb.

"Hey, look at this," I said to Peaches.

She was removing the sheet from the bed and went on with the task until she was finished. Only then did she look over.

"What about it?"

"It doesn't feel like a tomato any more," I said. "It's all toughened up. Here, feel it."

"I won't, if it's all the same to you," she said.

While Peaches remade the bed, I examined the transformed tomato under the lamp. Its color was the same, and it still looked like a tomato, except for the holes top and bottom.

"You wouldn't happen to have some kind of flexible tubing around, would you?" I asked her. "A hose?"

"There's a hose on the washing machine."

"Where's that?"

"In the kitchen closet. It's not hooked up."

"Mind if I borrow it?"

She gave me a very disdainful look, but no answer. I made my way through the dark to the kitchen, and here, under the light of a naked, weak bulb, found an old wringer-style washing machine with the hose I needed.

Next, I extracted the large can of tomato juice from the refrigerator. Finally, I searched for and found a big mixing bowl under the sink. I brought all these things back to Peaches' bedroom. The mixing bowl was icy against my naked stomach. My penis and the lengths of hose all bobbed together. I found Peaches had returned to bed and switched off the light. I turned it back on.

"Give me a break, would you?" Peaches said. "It's late. I just want to go to sleep and forget about everything."

"How about some string?" I asked her. "Strong thread would do."

"In my sewing basket, on my chest of drawers," she said. "But do it somewhere else, would you?"

"This won't take very long," I said. "If it works, I want you to see it."

I inserted the hoses into each end of the tomato and tied them tightly with the heavy thread. Then, with the mixing bowl on the floor to catch the runoff, I pinched off one of the hoses with a clothespin and poured the contents of the tomato juice can into the other hose. The tomato swelled somewhat as it filled with fluid, but it did not burst.

"Look here!" I called to Peaches. "Look at the pressure it can hold!"

Peaches wearily raised her head. The bedclothes were drawn up around her neck.

I squeezed the ripe bulb. Tomato juice spurted from the hose in a red jet.

"Wow," I said.

"Yeah, wow," Peaches replied.

"No, all kidding aside," I said. "This could be it! Let me show you what you're looking at. Here," I told her, pointing to the bottom hose, "is the vena cava, or the pulmonary vein, depending on which side of the heart we're talking about. And here," I indicated the top hose, "is the pulmonary artery or aorta. All of these vessels are usually O.K. in the patient and you just suture to them. Now here's what you put in." I pointed to the tomato. "It gets its power by being squeezed mechanically. I already have a power plant to do that, I told you about it. Now all I need are valves, and those are readily available. There are prosthetic mitral and aortic ball valves you can buy off the shelf that last in people up to five years without getting gummed up."

I squeezed the bulb a bit more sharply. The jet of tomato juice hit the ceiling this time.

"A tomato heart," Peaches said.

"More precisely, half a tomato heart," I said. "You need two of these working together."

"They'll go by on an assembly line, and a worker will jack off into each one," she said dreamily.

I brought the tomato heart under the light and examined it for leaks. There weren't any.

"Why does it have to be a tomato?" Peaches asked. "Why not a plastic baggie or something?"

"Because a baggie is a man-made thing, and the blood clots when exposed to it."

"Won't it clot when exposed to a tomato?"

"I don't know," I said. "No one's ever tried it. Maybe it won't. They're both biological things. Even the treatment I gave it was biological."

"That isn't blood in there now. It's tomato juice."

"I know," I said, and carried the tomato heart in its bowl out of the room.

In the kitchen, I poured the tomato juice down the drain and rinsed out the bowl. I had worked with blood before, in the final series of experiments on feather fiber. In fact, it had been these experiments which caused me to declare the invention a failure and to sell it to Neptune. I had obtained outdated whole blood from a hospital for my early set of trials. I had tried fresh animal blood, obtained from rats and guinea pigs, and finally small quantities of fresh human blood. This I had extracted from myself, making an incision in a peripheral vein, which I covered afterwards with a Band-Aid. The procedure was painful, but after I had done it several times, I was convinced it was safe.

Now I made preparations to do it again, finding a new razor blade and a package of bandages in a medicine chest above the bathroom sink. I brought these to my cot. The cutting and bleeding went easily enough, and I was careful to see that the wound bled directly into the tomato. I stopped the bleeding with my thumb and applied the bandage when the tomato was full. The volume of blood taken was rather more than I had ever drained out before. I began to feel dizzy and vaguely nauseated. There was only time to tie the tomato heart closed (it felt warm and active in my hand) and replace it in the mixing bowl before I lost consciousness.

T w e l v e

Henley was sitting on the cot beside my head when I
woke. The sun was full in the room: it was late morning.
Someone had put a pair of avocado pajamas on me. I was
covered by a light blanket.

"Are you awake, Daddy?"

"As far as I can tell."

"We found you when we came in late last night."

"I know. They were talking to me. I remember answering a lot of questions. It was terribly noisy."

"Maybe that was when Aké was examining you. He's a
doctor. He even practiced in Copenhagen before he gave it
up to come here. Wolf was terribly excited, but Aké said you
were O.K. Wolf thought you were trying to kill yourself."

"Oh, I wasn't," I said. "I was trying to *save* myself. It was part of an experiment."

"How do you mean?" Henley's jeans, near my head, had spots of blood on them. Mine, I supposed. I looked down on the floor. A red stain, wiped over, showed where the mixing bowl and its contents had been but were no longer.

"Wolf wanted to take you to the hospital, but Aké said they wouldn't do you any good, and they'd probably lock you up when they saw your wrist was cut. Especially if you couldn't speak French."

"Henley," I asked her, "what happened to the bowl that was on the floor right there?"

"I cleaned it out."

"What did you do with the tomato that was in it?"

"I put it in a garbage bag and left it out in the hall."

"Could you go now, quickly, and see if it's still there? I need to have it back."

She hopped up and ran into the kitchen. I heard the door which led to the back stairs open. Then shut. She came back.

"It's been taken away," she said.

"Where are things like that taken?"

"I don't know," she said. "I don't even know who takes them. I think the garbage is fed to pigs in the country."

Henley sat in a chair opposite my cot. Her hair must have been freshly washed this morning: it was lustrous. It wouldn't help to be angry with her, even though at this moment a pig in some Parisian suburb was in all likelihood chewing on my heart.

"I'm sorry, Daddy," she said. "I didn't know you wanted it saved. It made me feel bad to see it, all your blood like that. I just wanted it cleaned up."

"What did you think I was doing? Did you think I was trying to kill myself too?"

"I didn't know," Henley said. "I thought I'd wait and ask you."

"Do you remember what the tomato looked like when you threw it away? Were there brownish clots on it or was it clean?"

"Clean, I think," she said.

"I don't suppose you opened it up and looked inside."

"No," she said.

"That's what I really wanted to know, whether there were any clots inside."

"I'm sorry, I couldn't say."

"Don't you remember when I was experimenting with blood on the feather fiber? This was more of the same."

"I'm sorry I ruined it for you," Henley said. I saw that she really was. It was time to forget about it. Her face showed she was miserable.

"Please don't worry," I said. I held out my arms. She knelt by the cot and let me cradle her head. There were tears in her eyes. "Did it scare you?"

"Yes," she said. She wept, and I stroked her hair. "You were lying on the floor naked, and there was blood on you."

I brushed her hair back out of her eyes. With the back of my wrist, I gently wiped her cheek. Her back heaved in sobs. I held her for a while until she was calm again.

"I should have known it was only one of your projects," she said, letting her voice be a whisper. "But your face was so pale, and your expression was a million miles away. Like you'd given up."

I kissed her temple. "I think I've changed my mind," I told her, "about giving up."

Henley and I left the Annex late in the morning. I had made reservations for a one-thirty BEA flight to London. To eliminate the need for coming back to the Annex, I took my suitcase with me. With several hours to ourselves, we set out walking toward the river, deliberately not taking the Metro. The air was cool and fresh again today, and the sun bright; Henley said this was unusual for August.

In spite of the alert feeling of the weather, I was listless and groggy: I yawned often. Since the beginning of my illness, I've found myself yawning much more frequently. Silverman says its part of the syndrome, like the nocturnal dyspnea. A moving van stopped in traffic in the street, a door open in its side obscuring the giant block letters that spelled the name of the mover. I recognized this as a mechanical analogy of the yawns hiding my face, and I tried to suppress them.

We stopped to drink from a water fountain in a park. Henley drank first, gathering her hair in one hand and holding it out of the way as she bent forward. Some water splashed on the front of her sleeveless blue polo shirt. I waited for my turn. As I watched her, I felt pride in her health, in the snug and slender fit of her clothes, in her intelligence, in the fact that she was my child. The cold water coming up for her made two sounds simultaneously, like the horns on a fancy car. There was the faucet cry as it came past the foot pedal, and the splashing sound as it fell back into the cast-iron dish. When she was finished drinking, drops clinging to her chin gave back the radiance of the sunshine before she wiped them away.

As I drank, I became aware suddenly that she was gone.

I looked up. She had gone somewhere, it wasn't plain where. The sharp shadows cast by trees, their tops great wildernesses of leaves, left the ground and its grass almost in darkness at the edges of the park. In one of these shady places behind my back, a swing began to creak.

"Daddy," the swinger called.

As Henley pumped, and the amplitude of her motions increased, at first stray bits, then whole sheets of her hair lifted up and streamed away. They followed her like a veil. She pulled in her legs, then thrust them out and sat back deeply as the swing plunged and climbed. Her feet would drag on the ground if she failed to lift them. Soon she was moving so swiftly that her doe-like swoops were making a swishing noise. I finished drinking, then walked to the base of her swing and sat in the cool grass.

"Don't you want to swing, too, Daddy?" she asked, using a voice loud enough to reach me on the ground. "It's wonderful. You go shooting up, and you think you're going to run into that branch there. But you don't. It just twitters its leaves at you."

"I suppose I could try," I said.

I sat on the yellow seat of the swing next to hers. I pushed myself off with my foot, the way you would going out in a boat. I moved out, then back, with rusty sounds from above.

"This *is* fun," I said. But I didn't go as high and as fast as Henley.

"At the top," she said, pumping up again, "I stick my feet out and I can see the sun through my toes." Her sandals were lying in the dirt below.

We creaked back and forth, swinging together sometimes, but more often in different phases, five of her swings for four of mine. She slowed down to keep us more closely together.

"How would you like to tell me a story?" she asked. She rested her head against the chain, just above the point where her hand grasped it. I was surprised and charmed. *She still likes the things she's always liked.* It increased my hope, made our family stronger somehow to remember that Portia, the least sentimental of all of us, had said this.

"O.K.," I said. "What should the story be about?"

"Sex and adventure," Henley said.

"You never used to get stories about sex and adventure."

"I never knew how to ask for them."

We creaked back and forth, Henley grazing the dirt with her toes, as I looked for an appropriate idea to begin with.

"Once upon a time," I started, "a family from Massachusetts rented an old house on an island off the coast of Maine for the summer."

"I don't want this to be a true story," Henley said.

"It isn't. We never rented a house on an island, did we? Our house was on the shore."

"O.K., proceed," she said.

"Well, the island was so far away from the mainland that you could just barely see one from the other on a clear day. And of course, you couldn't when there was a storm. The family, which was a father, a mother, and a young girl, had been led to expect that theirs was the only house on the island by the real estate lady. This fact sounded particularly good to the father, who worked in a boiler factory and came home holding his ears every day."

"There isn't any such thing as a boiler factory any more," Henley said.

"No? I thought there was. Anyway, as I say, theirs was the only house on this island, or so they thought, until they explored the coast and encountered a high stone wall that cut the island nearly in half. Actually, they had no way of knowing what was on the other side, because the wall was so high and even extended out into the sea.

"The only way that food and supplies could reach the island was on the mail boat, which was under the command of a sour old fellow by the name of Captain Buzzard. The family asked Captain Buzzard about the wall, and although he denied any knowledge of it, he acted very uncomfortable at their mention of it and crashed into their dock with the mail boat as he was backing away."

"Captain Buzzard is a bit much," Henley said. "I mean, I think he's hamming up his part."

"Whose story is this, yours or mine?"

"Yours."

"Then just let me tell it my own way," I said. "You'll see in a minute that Captain Buzzard is an important person in this story. Now, shortly after the family discovered the wall, there was a giant storm, a hurricane really, that battered the rocks and laid the trees over for two days. The waves were so big and the noise of the wind was so great that the family couldn't sleep for all the frightening sounds. On the morning of the third day, the weather cleared and the family went outside. They roamed up and down the rocky coast, looking at the fallen trees in the woods and the debris on the beach. And then they came upon a beautiful young woman, unconscious in the sand, clad in only a flesh-colored life jacket."

"I was wondering when we were going to get to the sex," Henley said.

"Just wait," I told her. "The father carried this young woman, who had long red hair, up to the rented house, where she was put to bed in the guest room. For five days, she lay unconscious, barely moving in her sleep. They learned her name, or possibly the name of the ship she had been aboard, from a stencil on the life preserver: Eustacia. On the fifth day, she began to moan and cry out in her sleep, but she only just repeated one word over and over again."

"What was that word?" Henley asked.

"The word was 'diddle,'" I said. "Again and again, that's all she said, was 'diddle.'"

"This is great so far," Henley said, "But I think you'd better make it two or three days instead of five days she was unconscious, or else she'd be too weak to talk."

"O.K.," I said, "Three days. By that time, the ocean was calm enough for the mail boat to come in, and the family was anxiously awaiting it, since they were nearly out of food. Their hunger got so great they went out into the woods looking for edible plants and roots, and when they returned, the mail boat was at their dock, empty. As they approached the house, Captain Buzzard was seen leaving the rear door in great haste. Inside the girl was still unconscious."

"Was she still saying 'diddle?'"

"I'm not sure about that," I said. "I suppose not. Let's say she'd stopped. Just then, the engine of the mail boat started and it backed way from the dock at top speed. Whoever was running it was keeping down out of sight in the wheel-house. It backed all the way out onto the ocean, and didn't turn around and go forward until it was just a dot.

"After that, the family knew that they were on their own until someone, the real estate lady or some neighbor at home, noticed that they were out of communication with the mainland and came to investigate. The father caught fish from the dock, but as their other stores of food ran low, they had to search farther and farther into the woods for edible growing things. The girl was by this time sitting up in bed and eating, but claimed to remember nothing about her life prior to the time she was washed up on the beach.

"One morning, the father and daughter were foraging in the vicinity of the high wall."

"What was the mother doing?" Henley asked.

"She was in the house making root soup."

"Root soup?"

"Yes," I said.

"All this talk about food is making me hungry. Are you hungry?"

"I'm a little bit hungry," I said, "but I still don't feel very well, so I'm not really dying to eat."

"Let's walk in the direction of the river, and if we see a place to eat, we'll sit down. Meanwhile, you go on with the story."

"O.K.," I said. "The father and daughter were in the woods, near the wall. Then they noticed that in one place, where the wall went through a grove of trees, someone had chipped away at it with a chisel to form a ladder of sorts, stepping places by which the wall could be scaled."

Henley and I walked out of the park. My dusty suitcase was in my hand. On the street, the day's glare was at its peak. My watch, whose crystal reflected the blue sky, said it was near noon. Henley walked by my side, but sometimes we had to go single file to let people pass.

"And so they went over the wall," Henley said.

"Yes, they went over the wall, and at first they were disappointed because on the other side they found only more forest. But they wandered on, and eventually they came to an open field with hundreds of blueberry bushes in it. They had no trouble at all filling two big shopping bags they'd brought with blueberries."

"That's all there was on the other side of the wall? A blueberry patch?"

"No, there was something else, just wait and see."

"How about this place?" Henley suggested, indicating three or four tables outside of an inconspicuous café we were passing.

"Fine," I said.

We sat down. The waiter, a boy of fifteen or so, brought us menus under acetate. We both ordered big salads and the house wine. The fringe on the awning above our table jerked in the wind. The cool, steady wind and clear air gave the impression that we were at sea.

"Go on," Henley said.

"They found a path through the blueberry bushes which took them into the forest again at the other side of the field. The path took them up a hill which had a meadow at the top. From this meadow, they could see the whole island, including their house, which was now some miles away. They could see the entire shoreline of the island, including the wall, where it went off into the ocean on both sides. And in the other direction, down below them, perched on a cliff above the ocean, was a large old mansion."

"Aha," Henley said. She smiled.

The waiter came with our salads. He put them down on a nearby table while he arranged our silverware in front of us. Then he served us our meal.

"They walked slowly down the hill in the direction of the mansion. Near the foot of the hill, they encountered some old gardens, which were now grown over with weeds. But you could tell that they had once been really something. There was a rotted old gazebo with trellises on it where roses still bloomed."

Henley dug into her salad. I poured a half glass of red wine for each of us.

"As they got closer to the house, they saw that it was surrounded by another wall, but this one had a massive stone arch with an iron gate, and the gate was open. Above the gate, in iron scrollwork letters, was a name: D'Iddle with an apostrophe."

"Oh, you mean D'Iddle with an apostrophe?" Henley asked. She made the apostrophe in the air with her finger.

"Yes."

"That's funny," she said. "That's really pretty funny."

"That's also all I'm going to say until after lunch," I said. "I don't want to talk with my mouth full."

As we ate, our steel table rocked on the cobblestones as one of us or the other put our forks into our salads. I put my napkin into my lap and noted with satisfaction that it was a nice pressed cloth one, not the paper type usual in America.

"When do you have to be at the airport?" Henley asked.

"My plane leaves at one-thirty, so I guess I should be there by one."

"We should leave after we finish here, then," she said. "I wish you didn't have to go so soon."

I ate my salad. "Maybe you can come home and see me this year," I said. "At Christmas, perhaps. Do you get a break then?"

"Not really," Henley said. "The company has a production."

"Well, next summer, then."

I was instantly remorseful for having brought up the subject of when we would be together again. Next summer was far away, there was a lonely year in the interval.

And of course, I might get worse in the meantime. Our café table rocked as if it were on a wallowing deck. I had eaten enough: I abandoned my salad and let Henley have the table, which then came onto an even keel.

"Are you going to see Mother again before you go back?"

"Yes," I said.

"Why?" she said. "I mean, isn't it just a punishment?"

"Oh, no," I said. "The opposite."

Henley finished the last few leaves in her bowl.

"I think both of us are a lot stronger now," I said. "She's obviously much stronger. She didn't really tell me where she was going, you know, when she left. I think she was afraid to, or she didn't know. Now we can talk about what she wants quite matter-of-factly. I think maybe she's had the experience she wanted to have in running away."

"I wouldn't be surprised," Henley said. "Although, I must say I never know how Mother's going to play her shots. That Dawlish guy bores me to death. I couldn't spend five minutes with him."

"He's terribly tense."

"He's fucked up," Henley said. "But that doesn't make him very special. I don't see why Mother stays with him."

"He leaves her alone," I said. "Or at least I got the impression he does."

"That's not much," Henley said.

"He keeps her from being by herself in the city."

"As far as I know," Henley said, "He only did one thing for Mother, and that was to take her in when he found her wandering around starving in a railway station. That was the first and last help he ever was to her."

"She was in a railway station?"

"That's what I understand," Henley said. "It was last winter."

"Who told you that?"

"Dawlish himself. He was having a little private talk with me. He wanted me to take Mother to Paris with me. I suggested it, but she said no. I don't think she'd like living in the Annex, anyway."

"When was this? When you visited them last month?"

"Right," Henley said. "I've only been there that one time."

The waiter took away our salad plates and brought us coffee.

"So Dawlish wanted to get her out?"

"That's what he said to me."

"Did he give you any reason?" I asked.

"He said it was costing too much money to feed both of them."

"But I was sending Portia money."

"He also said his landlord is a Pakistani who doesn't approve of him having a white lady living with him."

"Ah," I said. "Now, that's a piece of news."

We sipped our coffee. It was cooling rapidly in the breeze. I noticed for the first time that this street was reasonably quiet, certainly by comparison with many of the other parts of the city I'd seen. Through the window looking into the restaurant, we could see our own reflections, and behind them, the dim silvery image of the young waiter serving at the tables inside.

"What are you going to do, Daddy?" Henley asked me.

"I'm going back to Boston and work on my new idea."

"That's fine," Henley said, "but I didn't mean that. I mean what are you going to do about Mother?"

"I'm not sure yet," I said. But even then, I was beginning to have a plan.

Thirteen

After our meal, we caught a cab to the airport. I never finished the story. We had both forgotten about it. The drive to the airport seemed shorter than it had on my arrival, but this impression may have been colored by the time of day and the traffic.

I joined a line at the BEA counter to pick up my ticket and check my bag. Henley and I waited together behind some other Americans. We all shoved our suitcases forward with our feet when the line moved ahead. There were many young people there, and although they carried guitar cases instead of bags, they shoved them forward with their feet like the rest of us.

"It's not very much fun seeing people off at airports," Henley said. "At least at a steamship dock, you get the salt air and the creaking wood and the foghorn blowing when the ship goes away. Here it just sounds like a million vacuum cleaners."

"Maybe it would be more fun if I bought you something," I said.

"You already bought me the blouse, for which I thank you very much. And you gave me that sumptuous loan."

"It isn't really a loan. You don't have to pay it back."

"Bullshit, Daddy," she said. "I wouldn't have taken it if I wasn't going to be good for it later. I wouldn't need it in the first place, except that money is the only thing Henri can ever force himself to be serious about."

I took my turn at the head of the line. The ticket agent weighed my bag and put a tag on its handle. I paid for my ticket with the English currency Neptune had given me. I received directions to my gate and was told that the airplane was already boarding.

"I want you to take this," I said to Henley, giving her a twenty-franc note, "and buy a bottle of whatever that wine was we were drinking at your place. Present it with my compliments at the table tonight."

"This is too much," she said. "This will buy four or five bottles of that stuff."

"Buy four or five, then," I said. "Tell them all goodbye for me. It was a pleasure to meet them all. They made me feel good."

"I'm sure they'd say the same thing. They really liked you. Especially what you did on the stage yesterday. I heard them talking about it."

We walked to the gate. It wasn't very far. Here there was another line, but it was shorter and faster moving than the one at the ticket counter. I delayed joining it until Henley would have to leave me.

"I'll come back," I said. "It was a mistake to put off coming to see you this long. I was staying in Boston waiting for a kind of equilibrium, but it wasn't coming."

"Oh, you can't do that," Henley said. "There isn't any such thing as equilibrium. As I like to say, things are always either getting better or worse. And that's fine." We looked at each other directly. I was amazed that Henley knew such an important thing and I didn't. I couldn't have asked her before. And now, unfairly, it was time to leave.

We looked at each other directly.

"I love you, Daddy," she said.

"I know. It's the best thing that ever happened to me."

"Tell Mother I'm sorry I was such a pill when I visited her."

"I'm sure she isn't worried about it," I said. "I have to go now." I bent down and kissed her left ear. She kissed me back.

"Goodbye," she said.

By this time, the line had all moved through. I showed my ticket to the man at the gate, who waved me by. Before I went through the doors to the airplane, I looked back, but Henley was already gone.

The flight across the channel was rough. The cool air which had slid in an uneven breeze through Paris became a clear-weather gale above the ocean. Whitecaps and blowing spindrift were visible on the surface of the sea, even at the altitude we were flying. All the children aboard the aircraft, which was an otherwise-comfortable Trident, howled through the whole flight, and several people were ill. The stewardesses had only begun their tea service when the seat belt sign came on and remained on until we landed in England.

The BEA bus took me to the air terminal in London. The same clock on the wall above the lunch counter where I had eaten three days ago said that the time was nearing three o'clock. I would have to hurry. I carried my bag out on the street to the taxi stand and got in a cab. As we moved through the busy streets, I sorted through the coins in my pocket, separating the English from the French. I brought out three two-shilling pieces and nested them together in my palm: this should be the fare plus tip. As the cab pulled up in front of Portia's blue door, I saw that I would have to add another shilling to the pile to exceed the meter reading by an equitable twenty percent.

Inside, I climbed the steps to the second-floor hall and knocked at Portia's door. There was no answer. A slight modification of my intentions was now called for. I continued up the steps to the third floor, the top of the building, and knocked at the door where we had borrowed the mattress I had slept on previously. The thin, young Pakistani student who owned the mattress came to the door. He said he didn't know where Portia was, but he presumed Dawlish was still at his job.

"It's Dawlish I'd really like to speak with at the moment," I said. "Can you tell me the address of his office?"

The young man was silent. He smiled in discomfort and embarrassment. "I don't know it," he said.

"Look," I said, "it's rather important. I don't mean to harm him, you know."

"You are the husband of the American lady."

"Sure," I said. "But that doesn't make me dangerous. This is the civilized world, after all. I have an urgent matter to discuss with Dawlish, to our mutual advantage. I'm sure he'll thank you later for giving me the information. Look, here's a sixpence. Why don't you go to the telephone downstairs and call him. Tell him I'd like to meet him after work."

The student took my sixpence and went down the stairs, sliding his thin, chestnut-colored hand down the banister. I amused myself looking out of the window above the landing at the clay smokeless chimney pots of neighboring buildings while he was gone. Portia would be at the swimming pool. I wondered where it was. She had given me the impression it was nearby. I visualized her in her nylon tank suit, springing into the water from the pool edge. She is not particularly interested in diving, and rarely uses the board. I have never seen her frolic in a pool; it's all business. She writes out the work she has planned for herself in an appointment book she carries in her purse. The routines of each day are varied, but the full workout amounts to about the same effort each time. I'm not sure which of her coaches taught her to keep track of her progress like this, but I'm certain it's something she was taught. I looked at my watch. Three forty-five. She would be coming back soon. Given the change in plans, it would be awkward to meet her on the stairs.

Dawlish's friend returned.

"He says he'll meet you at a pub around the corner from his office. The name of the pub is the Elephant and Castle. I've written the address for you."

"Thanks very much," I said. "What time?"

"Six-thirty."

This left me enough time to check into a hotel, which I accomplished on my third try. The city was crammed with visitors this time of year, and accommodations were hard to find.

F o u r t e e n

It was after nine when I returned to my hotel in Montague Street, a place called the Beaumont. The front was painted two shades of green. There were three floors, and the front rooms looked across the street to the British Museum. The old wood-and-glass front door was locked, as I had been told it would be after eight o'clock, but my room key opened it. Inside, the entrance hall carpet ran forward under a second set of doors, then branched right and left into the sitting and dining rooms, and up the stairs. The brass push plates in the doors were polished. Mirrors hung in the entrance hall and stairwell so that you could see yourself walking up the stairs. Every one of the treads creaked as I stepped on them.

My room was on the second floor at the front, reached over a further continuation of the carpet. The door opened into a short hallway. I closed the door behind me, entered the room, and sank down onto one of the two beds. The mirror on the wall opposite showed me the light fixture on the ceiling, its two bulbs cool on the outside but white-hot at the center, like a double star.

I took my wallet and stray pieces of English money out of my pocket. Dawlish had let me pay for our beer and steak-and-kidney pies. I had even bought him a little ten-pack of cigarettes, after he had asked me for a butt and it came out that I didn't smoke. Without Portia, I found him more relaxed, and therefore more attractive. After we had finished the business I came to discuss, we talked together very peacefully. His Hindu childhood had been filled with magic. In his father's house it had been necessary to put flour all around the edges of the floor near the walls so that the family might discover whether cobras had come in during the night. When it was determined that a snake had come in, the family was not allowed to disturb it, but could only watch the flour track each day to know when it had gone.

In the bathroom, which was at the end of the second-floor corridor, I locked the door and ran the tub full of warm water. The tub must have been six feet long. I entered the water, haunches first, a bit at a time, giving the water time at each stage to convince me to come farther. It was re-markably comfortable to be able to stretch out my feet and lie back, my head supported by the ceramic curve. I prefer bathtubs to showers; so does Portia, who washes often. In the farthest corner of the ceiling, unknown and unknowable English spiders had spun a beautiful silver construction that was now laden with drops of condensation, decorative presents to them from the bath with my compliments.

Later, in my bed, I lay anticipating the next day and couldn't sleep. I put on the light and found myself reading, of all things, a car magazine left in a drawer of the bedside table by a previous guest.

In the morning, the two open windows facing Montague Street sent in raucous exhaust noises. Taxis evidently use the street as a shortcut from somewhere to somewhere else, and make the best speed they can over the stretch in front of the Beaumont. I had agreed to meet Neptune at Boscombe Down later that afternoon. I stepped out of bed and looked down into the street through one of the windows. The cool Scandinavian air had gone, leaving behind a high overcast which prompted some people in the street below to be carrying furled umbrellas. I opened my suitcase on the other bed and put on the cleanest clothes I had. In the bathroom, I washed my face, shaved, and brushed my teeth. This was the biggest overhaul my appearance had been given for several days, but I noticed in the mirror with dismay that not much change was evident.

I checked out with the lady who owned the hotel before going into the dining room for breakfast. There I was served by a French girl with shallow breasts and somewhat unattractive skin. When she brought me my breakfast, the toast was cold, but I didn't feel like arguing about it. I asked her where I might find a library with scientific books open that morning. She said she had no idea, but she knew that they had some books across the street at the museum. I thanked her and ate my meal. Each piece of heavy silverware was cold the first time I picked it up.

By ten o'clock, I was out on Montague Street, my bag in my hand, looking for an entrance to the grey museum buildings. A passerby told me to walk down the block to Great Russell Street, where the main entrance was.

Some people were stopped to watch something in the sky. I looked up, and with some effort because of the glare against the thin clouds, saw what they were looking at. It was Neptune's blimp, flying across the city to the south of us, perhaps over the Thames. The steady hum of his propellers was at a low note; he was flying slowly, almost hovering. I hadn't expected him to be over England this time of day, but he was obviously taking advantage of the detour in his route to do a little advertising in London. I watched him for several minutes, until he was almost out of sight among the chimney pots. I was just about to turn away when the electric sign on the side of the blimp came on. I could see letters moving electronically across the sign the way they do in Times Square, but I was too far away to read what they said.

When Neptune dipped behind a building, I went up the steps into the museum. The marble hall was vast and hollow. Crowds of people walking in various directions seemed to be warning each other out of the way with their clattering heels. With the assistance of a man in uniform, I found a library that was thought to have books on the natural sciences.

For a half hour, I searched the card catalog. I assembled a list of books on botanical subjects and ordered them up from the stacks. On the whole, I was disappointed, but part of this disappointment may be charged to the fact that I had only a vague notion of what I was looking for. I wanted to know, for example, if tomatoes could be grown to take a specified form. Would it be possible to grow them in a plaster mold, so that they had the desired heart shape when mature? I uncovered gardener's encyclopedias which showed me color illustrations of tomatoes and their common diseases. I found advice on the proper times of year for planting, the correct spacing interval, and what to do about weeding and fertilizing (I, of course, had an innovation to offer here), but there were never discussions of how to control their form, or for that matter, their function. Although I investigated all the books on my list, and even some technical papers that I found referenced in a current book, there was nothing useful. I discovered it impossible to even approach some of my questions in the available literature, such as whether or not tomatoes might be grown in blood.

The book stacks were grey, airless rooms as if the intention were to discourage the growth of any green things. When two hours had passed, and I realized that this search and others I might undertake in other libraries would turn up only further species names and tips for planting, I began to feel frustrated for the first time since the tomato heart idea had come to me. It seemed impossible, given the long human cohabitation with tomatoes, that no one had noticed before the strange transformation I had seen. Mine had been an unlikely experiment, to be sure, but even so, it seemed to me that there had been enough people and enough tomatoes around sufficiently long for the discovery to have been made.

On my way out of the library, a photograph on the wall caught my attention. I came closer and read that the sculpture shown in the photograph was Bernini's *Daphne and Apollo*, where Daphne, with Apollo's arms around her waist, is shown in the moment of transformation into a tree. At this instant, her body is still smooth and fair, and her skin is white, but in the next moment, it will take on the texture of rough bark. Only Daphne's fingers and toes, the most distant parts of any creature from the heart and therefore the coolest, have completed their transformation into leaves and shoots. Her feet have become roots, and are already disappearing down into the soil.

I spent several minutes staring at the beauty of Daphne's changing form, and even pulled up a chair to wade through the questions which occurred to me. Here is a form, once human, now becoming a plant: If myth considers it possible, can it be entirely impossible? The scientific literature, now to my back in its concrete archives, had nothing at all to say in favor of a generality between plants and animals, but here was the visible sight of it. A slip of the tongue more valuable than all the official communiqués. Apollo's face registers anguish, but perhaps his dismay is mistaken. The real truth could be that her substance endures, an animal heart in a living tree.

Out on Great Russell Street again, I found that it was nearly time for me to begin making my way toward King's Cross. The weather had not improved, but it was still not raining. I walked to Oxford Street, and there I ate a rather poor lunch in a restaurant where you sat on vinyl-covered benches. When I had paid for my meal, I went out onto the street to look for a taxi. Neptune's blimp was still moving slowly over the city, its electric sign bright and readable against the dark overcast. He was coming toward me, and I waited as he passed nearly directly over the spot where I was standing on the sidewalk. I could hear the sound of the engines and propellers over the street traffic, except when a bus passed, and saw the mooring ropes trailing from the nose. The electric sign began a new sequence, but it was difficult to read it because of the angle.

IRA...something...something

A message for me? He knew I had planned to be here today, but there had been no definite agreement. If it were a message for me, I should know what it said. He was moving off toward the west now, leaving me his big fins but practically no view of the sign at all. I waited until he turned north at the end of his leg. I crossed the street in the meantime in order to be able to keep him in sight. At last, when I had him in better view, the sequence was played again. I had been mistaken, it had nothing to do with me:

WRITE, WIRE OR CALL GOLDFARB'S...

And my concern had been over nothing more than reading an "A" for an "E." I left Neptune to his advertising activities and hailed a cab.

The taxi left me on the sidewalk in front of Portia's door. I ascended the front steps, opened the blue door, and looked in. There was no one in the hall or on the stairs. I climbed to the second floor. Still no one. The tree outside the landing window held fixed against the overcast. I knocked at Portia's door. I heard her footsteps coming toward the door, and then it was open.

"Oh, Ira," she said. "I didn't know you'd be here today." She was wearing a pair of blue jeans, somewhat like Henley's as a matter of fact, over her black nylon tank suit. "Come in," she said. "Dawlish is out doing the food shopping. I was just about to go practice at the pool."

I came in and put down my bag.

"I'm afraid there isn't anything in the house to offer you," she said. "Dawlish will be home in a little while. Maybe he'll bring some Indian bread we can have before dinner. Can you stay to dinner?"

"No," I said. "I'm taking the train to Salisbury in an hour. We leave from there to fly back tonight."

"*Salis*bury," Portia said. "That's a funny place to leave from."

"It's a long story," I said. "What I'd like to propose is that you come with me."

Portia was silent. She stood motionless. The position she was in must have some name or number in ballet: her weight was slightly more on one foot than the other, so that one foot was at a forty-five degree angle to the other, knees slightly bent, back straight (was it ever otherwise?), left hand down by the side, right hand still grasping the doorknob so that the line of the right arm was broken at the elbow.

"You think about it, I'll pack," I said.

I looked for her suitcases and spotted them peeping out from the top shelf of her wardrobe. I climbed up on a chair and took down one of the suitcases. It was the same old brown one Portia had been taking with her to swim meets when I first knew her. I opened it on her bed and began filling it with her clothes. Underwear went in first, on one side, neatly arranged. Next came skirts and trousers, and the few dresses Portia owned, which I found hanging from a hook in the wardrobe.

I uncovered a half-used box of paper underpants.

"Shall I put these in?" I asked her. She ignored the question and looked away. I took this answer to be in the affirmative, and found a neat little place for them in the suitcase. Her cloth coat went on top, and finished this part of the job. I snapped the locks and went up on the chair again for the other one.

Portia climbed up on the chair with me. Her breasts pressed against my arm. She took the suitcase from me and put it back on the shelf.

"Ira, I *can't* come home with you yet," she said. "You don't know this, but I was planning to come home in December. I had my mind made up, really, as soon as the fall competition schedule was over. But I'm *signed up*. And I know I can win."

"You can win in Boston, too." I said. "With me. I might even do a little winning myself." I took the suitcase down again.

"*No*, Ira," she said and seized the handle of the suitcase. We wrestled. The chair tipped. Portia nearly lost her balance, then wrenched the suitcase and in doing so pushed me. I flew off the chair and struck the floor in a cartwheeling gyration, skidding as I went, sliding nearly to the kitchen before I stopped.

I lay on my back. My heart raced. The edges of my vision were red. My shoulder and back hurt. Portia was still standing on the chair, a look of terror on her face. She brought the knuckles of one hand up to cover her lips. The suitcase dangled from the other hand.

I let my head fall to the side. I relaxed. Among the scintillations and points of color I saw real things: the legs of the kitchen table, Dawlish's bed, Dawlish's motor bicycle.

Portia made a little cry, but didn't move.

Slowly I got to my knees, and then eventually to my feet. My heart pounded. There was some pain in my chest, but the bruises on my shoulder and back served as distractions. I faced Portia again. She was still standing on the chair. I approached her. There were points of light coming between us, but I could see her clearly.

"Ira, I didn't mean for you to fall..." she said.

I grabbed her above the knees and picked her up. She rose in the air, stuck fast in my grip. Her torso stretched above my head; her pelvis was against my face. The suitcase dropped from her hand. It fell away and sprang open on the floor. Her hands beat like wings against the wardrobe doors, then the wall, then my shoulders as I carried her through the room. I flung her down on her bed. Invisible feelings, insensible pains heated me like a chimney fire. I made a fist and slowly brought it up under her chin. I sat beside her on the bed.

"What are you going to do?" she said. Her face was deathly frightened.

My still fist went on threatening her. We stared at each other directly. "I'm going to take care of you for the rest of your life," I said. "And you're going to take care of me. Until we get to be old people, and pass away."

My wrist, with its terrible fist, lay on her breast. The long U of her bathing suit neck made a lap for it to nestle in.

"Is that really going to happen?" Portia asked me.

"Yes," I said, "as far as I can tell."

Her eyes were wet. "I'd like to be taken care of," she said.

"Well, that's what I'm going to do," I said.

"You were lying down so much. You were so silent. I thought there was nothing I could do for you. Until you died. Then I'd have to come in and pull the sheet up over your face."

"It's not going to be like that," I said. "We won't abandon each other. We both quit too easily before."

"It was so frightening," she said.

"For me, too," I said.

"Sometimes, when you didn't speak for days, I thought you were hoping you could die and leave me alone," Portia said.

"I don't want to die quite yet," I said. "It would only be more loneliness. I'm going to rescue myself."

Portia took my fist in her hands and kissed it.

"I'll help you," she said. Her black hair lay in a deep vortex around her head and shoulders. I bent forward slowly and kissed her lips. It was as if we were plunging into each other.

But there were footsteps on the stairs. And then someone approaching the door, bringing out keys. The key was in the lock, and the doorknob was turning. I sprang up and put my shoulder to the door, to keep it from being opened. The doorknob shook.

"Who's holding the door?" It was Dawlish's voice.

"Go away and come back later," Portia called to him.

"The hell!" Dawlish cried. "This is my flat. You let me in!"

Portia got up from the bed and threw the bolt. It was now safe for me to release the door, which rattled like an old Ford.

Together we filled the remaining suitcase. Portia dashed about the apartment, adding shoes from under the bed, a hairbrush from the window sill, her hair dryer from the wardrobe.

"Should we stop and explain to him what we're doing?" she asked. He was pounding on the door.

"Do you want to talk to him?" I said.

He was bellowing, now, in rage.

"No, I guess not," she said.

"Then I'll just get him away from the door."

Dawlish's motorbicycle was parked in the same place I had left it several days earlier. I switched on the ignition, lifted the front wheel, and gave it a jerk. The engine caught immediately.

"Open the door," I instructed Portia.

She drew back the bolt and let Dawlish's fists do the rest. As the door flew open, I opened the throttle on the motorbike. The front wheel, which I held up at chest height, spun at a furious speed, like a whirling blade. I advanced on Dawlish, my horrible weapon sputtering and spewing blue smoke. He retreated, at first through the door, then down the stairs. I pursued him, holding the head of the angry machine in restraint, as if it were using its own will against its former master. Portia followed with the bags. We clattered and thumped down the front stairs, leaving the air heavy with oily exhaust. People shouted at us from the landings and the floor above (were they cheering?). If they shouted at us again in the street, we didn't hear. The roar of the motorbike accepted the challenge of every other sound and was victorious.

Once outside, I set the motorbike in the street. In a moment, Portia and I were aboard it. She held the bags on her lap astraddle the bar, and off we drove.

We roared down the street, taxis and buses flowing around us, people straining from the sidewalk and from car windows to see such a burden of passengers and luggage on one little machine.

Portia's beautiful hair rippled back past my ears.

"We'll have to send Dawlish a postcard," she said. "He should at least know where we leave the bike. Not that he cares."

But I feel quite sure he found it, perhaps even later that day, in the very place, outside Waterloo Station, where we had agreed I would leave it. And by then we were over the North Sea, flying toward the low, buoyant sun. Portia was being carried home like a prize.